P9-BZO-556

WITHDRAWN

4-24-00

BLACK MOUNTAIN

G. P. PUTNAM'S SONS/New York

Les Standiford

BLACK MOUNTAIN

This is a work of fiction. Names, characters, places, and incidents
either are the product of the author's imagination or are used
fictitiously, and any resemblance to actual persons, living or dead,
business establishments, events, or locales is entirely coincidental.

G. P. Putnam's Sons
Publishers Since 1838
a member of
Penguin Putnam Inc.
375 Hudson Street
New York, NY 10014

Library of Congress Cataloging-in-Publication Data
Standiford, Les.
Black Mountain / by Les Standiford.
p. cm.
ISBN 0-399-14584-2
I. Title.
PS3569.T331528B58   2000   99-32943 CIP
813'.54—dc21

Printed in the United States of America

1   3   5   7   9   10   8   6   4   2

This book is printed on acid-free paper. ∞

Book design and title-page photograph by Jennifer Ann Daddio

Thanks to Scott Waxman, for believing;
and to Neil Nyren, Jim Hall, and
Rhoda Kurzweil, for all the help.
I couldn't have done it without you.

THIS BOOK IS DEDICATED TO

KIMBERLY, JEREMY, HANNAH, AND XANDER.

AND TO PHIL SULLIVAN,

WHO TAUGHT ME ABOUT BOOKS . . .

AND ABOUT THE MOUNTAIN.

In the mountains, the shortest route is from peak to peak,
but for that you must have long legs.

—NIETZSCHE

BLACK MOUNTAIN

CHAPTER 1

AUGUST 29

ABSAROKA NATIONAL FOREST, WYOMING

Bright had been trailing the black Suburban for nearly thirty miles, ever since it had left the gun shop in Sheridan, something called Mighty Malcolm's Arsenal and Ordnance. August was nearly gone, now, but there'd been a boldly lettered sign still hanging in one of the shop's barred windows, red, white, and blue: HAVE A BLAST ON THE 4TH OF JULY—ALL HANDGUNS DISCOUNTED.

Patriotism, Bright thought. Always a useful concept.

Take those proclamations pasted to the bumper of the big vehicle up ahead. TAKE MY GUN, KISS MY BUTT. THE NRA'S FOR CANDYASSES. And another sticker featuring a rendering of a fist with the middle finger extended, which Bright wasn't close enough to read.

An actual hand appeared briefly at one of the passenger windows of the Suburban, and a can sailed back in the slipstream, jouncing onto the pavement. Bright felt it pop under his own wheels. He'd seen perhaps a dozen other cans sail by in the last hour.

They'd turned off I-90 onto the state highway several miles back, had passed through two wide spots in the road known as Ranchester and Dayton, then turned northward again just shy of a flyspeck called Burgess Junction. They were deep in the heart of the Bighorn wilderness, now, on a winding, ever-climbing, two-lane blacktop that would give out to gravel before long, somewhere above 9,000 feet, somewhere in a vast spread of peaks and pine near the Montana line, population per square mile steady at zero. Bright, having spent far too much of his adult life in human ant piles, the past several months in Hong Kong, the most recent in New York, found the prospect pleasing.

There had been an exotic game ranch up there once, a fact he had learned in the course of his considerable research. The Roosevelt Preserve, named with unabashed irony, it had sprawled across the shoulders of Black Mountain, the most formidable of those angry-looking peaks and one that had been sacred to the Lakota tribe, the original settlers of the area.

The Lakota once had hunted the area, too, but they had taken only what they needed for survival and had offered up apologies to their gods each time an animal had fallen. Things had changed, of course. The Lakota long since slaughtered, the few survivors displaced. For a time, their sacred mountain had become a place where world-class high rollers had come to stalk ibex, gazelle, bison, bighorn sheep.

Were one to pay enough, Bright mused, one might have shot oneself a rhino up there, chased after a snow leopard with an automatic weapon, tracked down some bewildered elephant too old for the circus or stolen from some zoo, finished it off with a bazooka or a Sidewinder missile, whatever turned the hunter in oneself on.

The ranch had finally gone under, but there was talk of what storybook creatures had escaped or been left behind and were still roaming that far-flung wilderness. All of them fair game, free game, now, for the intrepid hunter, and for what seemed to be the freelance expedition such as that traveling the lonely road just ahead.

Time to bring that party back to its senses, Bright thought. Time to remind them how careless men can be. He nudged the accelerator of the big Ford Expedition, brought his window down, and reached to place the magnetic lamp onto the roof. It wasn't actually a policeman's light, of course, just as the uniform and the siren belonged to no jurisdiction, but they would help him get the job done.

At first, the Suburban ignored the flashing blue light, but Bright had expected that. He nicked the siren a couple of times, then held it, its unearthly squawks and whoops doubling and redoubling off the deep canyon walls.

Another mile, and the Suburban finally slowed, then bumped down grudgingly onto a turnout a hundred feet or so above the stream that sawed with timeless patience at the canyon floor below. Bright had turned off the siren but allowed the flasher to continue its whirl as he got out.

The moment he emerged into the still air, the heat struck at him. The better part of two miles up, but it was ovenish hot, as close and as hot here, it seemed, as it had been on the plains below. What kind of hunting weather was it, anyway?

"Some kind of problem?" It was a burly man who addressed him, the driver of the Suburban stepping down onto the gravel, so quiet Bright could hear the crunch beneath the man's spit-polished boots. Five-eleven, maybe six feet, a close-shaved head the shape of a concrete block, no discernible neck. With a massive chest above a formidable gut, he went perhaps 240, and Bright, himself six-two, his 200 pounds easily concealed in the loose uniform he wore, knew what it would feel like to hit him.

"Please take your hands out of your pockets," Bright told him evenly.

The man glanced down, then back inside the open compartment of the Suburban, rolling his eyes.

Bright heard something spoken inside, an answering guffaw of laughter. There were four of them altogether: one standing by the road in front of him, three hidden behind the smoked windows of the Suburban. Convinced he'd taken enough time to make his point, the driver took his hands out of his fatigue-fashioned pants and opened his palms to Bright.

"You worried I was gonna shoot you?" the man said. He offered a smile that came across as a leer.

Bright's own expression was neutral. "I'd like to have the others out of the truck," he told the man.

"What the hell's this about?" the driver said, taking a step toward him.

Bright didn't back away, simply held up his hand. Something in the gesture must have communicated itself to the man. He gave Bright an exasperated glance, then turned to the open doorway. "He wants you to get out," the man called.

A chorus of groans and muffled curses. The door nearest Bright swung open, and a tall man with a camouflage cap mashed atop his unkempt dark hair got out, kicking a beer can onto the gravel.

Hamm's, Bright noted. From the land of sky-blue waters. They were driving a $40,000 vehicle, drinking special-of-the-week beer. Possibly it appealed to their proletarian instincts.

The tall man looked at Bright. "He ain't been drinkin'," he said, jerking his thumb at the driver.

Bright nodded, as if it mattered. Then two others, the first a younger-looking, pseudomilitary version of the driver, and the second—something of a surprise to Bright—a stocky, light-skinned black man in jeans and a T-shirt, emerged around the back of the Suburban.

"What kind of cop are you?" the younger man said, and Bright assumed from his voice that he was the driver's son.

And a fair question, Bright thought. His vehicle was unmarked, his uniform, such as it was, unadorned. Pale green canvas trousers, a matching shirt, a badge that seemed vaguely official in its shape but offered no explanation as to his affiliation.

"Forest Service," Bright said. "I noticed your erratic driving."

"And I'm a Chinese aviator," the young one said. He glanced at his father. "This isn't any traffic cop."

"Take it easy, Simms," his father said.

"You mind if I just have a look in the back?" Bright said. Unnecessary, really. He'd had a look while the group had shopped at Mighty Malcolm's. They'd brought along everything he was interested in already. Whatever they had added there would be a bonus.

"You got a warrant?" This from the tall man, an unlikely-looking litigant.

"That why you stopped us, to have a look in the back?" the driver said. He affected calm, but there was new color flushing that close-cut scalp.

The black man had been staring closely at him. Bright noticed that the man's nose was unnaturally flattened, that a fine crosshatching of scars thickened the tissue above each eye. Maybe that explained what he was doing with this crew of self-appointed militia. Take enough punches, your natural enemies might seem to be allies.

"This fellow is a long way from home," the black man said abruptly.

There was something forlorn, something resigned, in the way he said it. Or perhaps it was just the shadow of the great mountain that sobered him. Either way, Bright thought, he'd sensed the truth of what was about to happen.

"Yeah, well, let me just get my license, Officer," the driver said, turning toward the cab of the Suburban.

The black man also had turned, and was heading around the corner of the Suburban when Bright withdrew the pistol from the holster at his belt. The first shot took the black man in the back, just beneath his left shoulder blade. He staggered forward, spine bowed as if he'd been kicked, then pitched over the side of the canyon.

The driver was turning with a pistol upraised when Bright shot him twice in the chest. He went backward into the cab of the Suburban, squeezing off a round that blew through the roof with a whang. The roar of the unsilenced shot echoed again and again off the narrow canyon walls.

Meantime, the driver's younger double was bent over, scrabbling for a pistol sheathed in an ankle holster. Bright shot him squarely in the top of his shaven scalp, and the young man fell back into a sitting position, his head lolling against the side of the Suburban as if he had had just too much beer and hot sun to bear.

The tall man had bolted around the back of the truck with an agility that seemed surprising for his awkward stature. Bright knew he'd be going for something inside the vehicle. Instead of pursuing the man, he stepped over the inert form of the young man before him and slid into the backseat, just as the opposite door was swinging open.

Bright kicked hard, heard the surprised grunt from the other side of the door. The man would have been yanking that door open with desperate force. Bright's kick was all it took. The tall man flew backward, lost his grip on the door handle, and sailed out into space, his arms windmilling. Bright caught a glimpse of his surprised face, was on through the passenger compartment in time to see the man land on the rocks below, his hands upflung in permanent surrender.

All done, well done, Bright found himself thinking. Then felt something grip his ankle, felt his foot fly from under him.

Stunned, he caught a glimpse of the face of the black man as he went down hard on his back. Bright felt his breath fly from him, felt his hand bang against the side of the Suburban, heard his pistol clatter away in the gravel.

The black man, his face twisted up in pain, was pulling himself up over the lip of the cliff, now, his gaze on the pistol, which had come to rest a few feet away. There was no question who would reach it first.

He saw the man's hand close on the weapon, saw the look of satisfaction on his face as he swung it toward him. Still gasping, Bright swept his hand through a skiff of gravel, stinging the man's face and raising a cloud of dust between them.

The black man cursed, and squeezed the trigger. Bright heard the familiar chuff of his own pistol, then a great, odd sigh from behind him, the sound of one of the Suburban's huge tires deflating in an instant. The black man was wiping the grit from his eyes with one hand, steadying himself for a second shot, when Bright braced himself against the flattened wheel and drove his heel against the man's forehead.

The man tottered, but clearly he had taken harder shots. He was bringing the pistol down once more when Bright kicked him again, this time high on the chest, where a bright stain had blossomed on his shirt. The man groaned and fell backward, one hand clutching at his wound, the other locking on to the leg of Bright's billowing trousers.

Bright kicked him again in the chest, then a third time, but though the man's eyes dimmed in pain, his grip on Bright's leg held firm. Bright slung one arm backward, clawing for a hold on the deflated tire with one hand, reaching for his belt with the other. His feet were sliding in the loose gravel, struggling for purchase like dream appendages. He yanked hard at the clasp of his belt, tore at the fastener of his waistband, his zipper.

He rolled onto his back, forced his shoulders hard against the wheel of the Suburban, kicked once more, this time giving it everything. He arched his hips off the ground with his follow-through, felt the cloth of his pants peel down his legs in an instant, felt weightlessness for a moment, then heard the man's cry as he sailed off into space. Bright's trousers were still clutched in his hand, flapping above him like some faulty parachute.

A tree limb jutting from the cliff tore the fabric from the man's hands and flipped him, end over end, toward the stream below. Had it been a true river, the man might have had a chance. Instead, he went head-down into water that might have been a foot deep, the apotheosis of a Do Not Dive Here warning. The crack rose to Bright as if two great stones had been clapped together.

Bright got to his feet, breathing heavily, and stared down at the crumpled figures below. After a moment, he retrieved his pistol, then went around to the other side of the Suburban to be certain there were no more surprises waiting.

The canyon had regained its former quiet. Heat waves shimmered above the mute asphalt road. No hum of sixteen-inch tires, no clack of cans tumbling toward the steep shoulders, no raucous, steel-edged laughter. Bright smelled the tang of pine in the still air. A pair of jays swooped overhead, their cries a harsh counterpoint to an otherwise peaceful scene.

The man who had been driving the Suburban lay half in, half out of the cab, his pistol clutched rigidly in his hand. The one Bright had taken for the driver's son still sat upright against the side of the truck, his porcine eyes bloodshot and protruding, a bottle fly making its way down the bridge of his nose, where a trickle of scarlet had dried.

Bright glanced at his watch, checked the angle of the sun, let his breath out in a sigh. He would have to find a way down that cliff and scale it again, would have to change a sizable tire, and so much else.

It was his own fault, of course. The matter could have been handled simply, with far less risk. But he had allowed himself an inexcusable breach of caution, given his line of endeavor and his considerable experience. Was boredom to account for it? Some lapse attributable to such thin air? He might be getting too old for this line of work, he thought. Perhaps he would have to start picking his jobs with more care.

He glanced out over the tops of the pines clinging to the roadside canyon, toward the distant line of peaks. Maybe it *was* the mountain, he thought, maybe some lodestone deep inside its mass, some essence that tugged at the workings of any man's inner compass. The Lakota had died, but not because they were stupid about such things.

He opened his hands to the mountain, bowed his head briefly. He had no idea if the Lakota had behaved that way, but he offered up his apology anyway. *This is what I must do.*

And then he turned to regard the men on the ground beside him and shook his head, driving superstition from his mind. They had died, he had not. He would not be so careless again. He had accomplished what he'd set out to do, and he could go on to the next step of the plan, now.

He bent down to pry the pistol from the hand of the man who'd been driving the Suburban, removed its clip, jacked the remaining round from the chamber. He was about to turn his attention to the arsenal in the back of the vehicle, when he thought of something.

It took him a moment—it was always difficult undressing a corpse—but it turned out that the pants fit perfectly. He tucked in his shirt, then glanced down at the man who had been so fond of his weapons.

Bright bent down, applied his lips to the tips of his fingers, and tapped the rigid buttocks of the driver. Acknowledge the spirit of your victim, was that not the Lakota way?

"Take my gun, kiss my butt." Bright nodded. He had his equipment, now; he had the bodies of the men upon whom everything would one day be blamed. All that remained, then, was the work itself. So he rose and began to do it.

CHAPTER 2

CENTRAL PARK

LABOR DAY

"NOW, I have not heard from the president lately. . . ." The sonorous voice boomed from the massive loudspeakers and was almost immediately swallowed by a wave of appreciative laughter from the holiday crowd that filled Sheep Meadow.

Fifty thousand of them, give or take, Corrigan thought. Almost as many as Simon and Garfunkel might get, though those would be paying customers, of course. He doubted many of the folks sprawled out there in the bright late-summer sunlight would have spent very much just to listen to Fielding Dawson.

The only reason Corrigan was there, for instance, was that he was getting paid. Then again, he supposed you could say Governor Dawson was getting paid, too. All those potential votes, all those cameras working, it'd have to pay off, if the governor ended up making his move, that is.

"This man, he is good," Rollie Montcrief said at Corrigan's shoulder. Montcrief was only six months out of the police academy and was still enthusiastic about a lot of things. Even the fact that he'd been lot-toed into the Transit Authority hadn't fazed him. "Hey, I could have ended up with Housing, man. Every night working the projects."

True enough, Corrigan thought, watching a father chase down a toddler racing across a grassy swale. The duty could have been worse.

Technically, he and Montcrief were members of an equivalent public agency, with a comparable pay scale, benefits, and the like, but everyone knew that despite all the talk of upgraded images, better equipment, and boosted morale, of the three police forces—Housing, Transit, and NYPD—only the latter were truly considered cops.

Corrigan stepped forward, caught the toddler before he could reach the fascinating trash can he had his eyes on, and lifted him up to the grateful father. "Thanks," the father said, hustling back toward his spread blanket with his child tucked under his arm.

Corrigan felt a vague stickiness on his hands, and wiped his palms on the back of his trousers without looking. Some things were better left unknown, he thought. Meantime, Fielding Dawson must have delivered another zinger up there, for the crowd was laughing again.

Corrigan had missed it. He'd suddenly found himself thinking of his own father, had been wondering with a pang how many errant children his old man had delivered back into the arms of a parent. One of the many little things they'd never had a chance to talk about.

His old man had been a real cop, one of the city's finest, and though Tom Corrigan had never voiced his disappointment while he'd been alive, Corrigan knew it had hurt him to see his son a mere cave cop. "We should be happy, Richie-boy, happy you're any kind of cop at all, what with the eye and all."

That line, with a downcast gaze and a stretch for another splash of Bushmills, that was as close as his father had ever come to voicing his real concerns, Corrigan thought as he gazed out over the crowd, about as close to an apology for his part in the accident as the man had ever come. And nothing to be done about that, now; even though Corrigan, four years on the force, had applied for a transfer, was working toward his bachelor's, was hoping that this time the doctors might be willing to overlook the issue of an old eye injury for a veteran officer and all. His old man was dead and gone, and even the wearing of the blue could never bring him back.

Nothing really wrong with his eye these days, anyway, Corrigan thought, nodding idly, barely glancing at his chattering partner. Nothing that affected his work. He could see just fine, the only real lingering effect of the injury a certain flattening of his depth perception, a slight washing out of distance. It was something he'd tried to forget, something he'd just as soon not think about.

Right now, for instance, he could see what he needed to see just fine. Governor Dawson up there on stage, doing his thing, all the happy people spread out on the fields beyond, listening with one ear and enjoying life. Just like Corrigan and Montcrief, happy to be goofing, for as long as it lasted, the two of them standing just beyond the west wing of the temporary stage, soaking up sun, backs to the stone wall that separated them from Central Park West and the subway station entrance that they'd been assigned.

Once the governor finished up, Corrigan and Montcrief would be among the gauntlet shielding Dawson, escorting him down the steps of the station to a rendezvous with a special downtown train: a big-shot express straight to the World Trade Center, where he'd address yet another gathering meant to help propel the as-yet-unannounced candidate into the thick of the race for the presidency.

After they had Dawson and the rest of the prominences safely tucked away, things would go more or less back to normal: He and Montcrief would spend the rest of the shift back in the ozone-laden caves, doing what they could to lend order to the chaos sure to come when the families started home. But right now they could take advantage of some rare paid time up top, out in the fresh air, sun on their faces. It had to be good for them both, even though they had to listen to Fielding Dawson's bullshit, even though Corrigan couldn't shake the feeling that in their distinctive commando-styled sweaters they stood out like a couple of cave fish tossed unaccountably to the surface of the earth.

Nobody was paying any attention to him and Rollie, however. All eyes were on Dawson, up there on the big platform, his silver mane so prominent, so shiny, you could probably spot him on the moon, flattened depth perception or no. The governor had his arms raised like some television preacher, turning this way and that to the still-roaring crowd.

Larger-than-life Fielding Dawson, an ambitious attorney who had parlayed a record as an outspoken member of the state legislature and a marriage to wealthy socialite Elizabeth Richardson into the governorship, was a curious mixture of pull-yourself-up-by-your-bootstrap-isms and Kennedy-esque concerns for the common welfare. He had not exactly broken ranks with the lame-duck president, but he had taken enough shots at Washington to endear himself to the cynical New York voter and, apparently, to sufficient numbers of the voting populace elsewhere. The world was aching for a hero, that's what Corrigan thought. And it seemed that's what Dawson intended to be.

"He talks the talk," Corrigan said grudgingly.

"And *she* walks the walk," Montcrief said. He'd already lost interest in matters political and was nodding at a young woman in a yellow halter top and skin-tight pants switching past them toward a line of Porta Pottis. She cast a sidelong glance at Montcrief, seeming to add an extra jounce to an already energetic motion.

"Not bad," Corrigan said.

"'Not bad'?" Montcrief said, his hand to his heart. "I am dying, here."

"Don't die while you're with me," Corrigan said. "I don't need the paperwork."

"That one could kill us both," Montcrief said, probably loud enough for her to hear if it hadn't been for Dawson's voice, finally carrying on.

"Now, *if* the president *had* called me," Dawson continued, the plosives blasting out of the speakers with a force that made Corrigan happy they were in the wings, "I would have told him that all his recent troubles could be traced to a simple source. . . ."

"We know what *that* is!" a heckler bellowed over several other catcalls.

Dawson smiled, again holding up his hands for quiet. "I'm serious, now," he called. "I would have reminded him why he had been elected in the first place. I would have reminded him that there is vast, unfinished business before us."

He paused and swept his gaze over the crowd. "We need, once and for all, to enact strong gun-control legislation, and we need to rededicate ourselves to the preservation of the natural environment," he added, in brief reference to the two issues that he had hammered on since he'd taken up residence in Albany. He jutted his formidable chin toward the crowd to finish. "I would have reminded him that he was sent to Washington to lead, not to try to please everyone . . ."

Dawson broke off as another cheer erupted. "*You* do it, Governor," the same heckler bellowed, and Corrigan wondered for a moment if the guy might be a plant.

"You the man!" the guy added. Sounded like the same asshole in the background at all the golf tournaments.

"I'm weighing all the options," Dawson called out over a general roar of approval. "I'm going to take a much-needed vacation, out West, where I can get out of the eye of the storm for a few days. But I assure you that I will make a decision sometime in the next few weeks."

More cheering, then, and Montcrief was shaking his head. "Why don't he just say the word?" he wondered. "Why not just come out and run?"

Corrigan shrugged. "It's always better when they come to you, Rollie. Like that *chiquita* you were looking at."

Montcrief cut his glance toward the Porta Pottis. No sign of the girl in the yellow outfit, but Montcrief nodded anyway, a smile crossing his handsome features. With his Latin-lover looks, he'd never had any problem getting the girls to come to him, Corrigan thought, and wasn't that a nice quality to have? It was not so easy for himself: He might have been born and bred in Brooklyn, a half dozen miles from where Rollie had grown up, but with his reddish-brown hair and fair complexion, he'd long ago pegged himself as a poster child for Midwestern life. Girls looked at Rollie, they probably had immediate notions of romance and intrigue; with Corrigan it was probably more like "ear of corn."

He turned back to the stage, then, his attention drawn by something he'd sensed more than focused on at first. He saw what it was, now, though. A tall guy there, approaching the back of the stage, apparently having emerged from the tangle of trees and underbrush along the boundary of the park, a place where the terrain rose up sharply to the north.

"My *chérie amour*," Montcrief was saying at Corrigan's shoulder. Probably the girl had finally popped out of one of the toilets.

"Look here," Corrigan said, his gaze fixed on the tall guy, nudging Montcrief with his elbow.

The guy was at least six-six, maybe more, and was moving awkwardly but intently toward the back of the stage, like a big water bird wading toward something enticing in the shallows. The temperature outside was probably nearing eighty, but the guy had a knit watch cap mashed down over his ears, a long overcoat flapping from his skinny frame, and what looked like knitted gloves on his hands, with the fingers cut out. Hard to get a fix on the guy, really, because everything about him—his clothing, his features, his entire aura—was indistinct, smudged.

"Looks like one of ours," Montcrief said as he turned.

"That's my guess," Corrigan agreed.

The very image, Corrigan thought, of one of the many who lived in the underground, moving from platform to platform, from maintenance tunnel to maintenance tunnel, kept on the move by Corrigan and the rest of the troops, one of their principal occupations in the course of a day, really, and a hopeless task it was. Keep the legion of the homeless moving, that's all they could do. Like setting off a bug bomb in your own apartment, which only sends the things you don't want to see scurrying into the hidey-holes next door.

"What's he got in his hand?" Montcrief was asking, but Corrigan was already on the move.

Fielding Dawson must have just delivered a humdinger, Corrigan was thinking as he ran, for the crowd was roaring, now, overwhelming anything that had come before, and the brass band up on the stage had erupted into a rousing fanfare.

"Hey, you!" Corrigan cried at the tall man bearing down on the stage. "Hold it! Police officer!" But his words were swallowed in the din.

There *was* something in the guy's hand, he saw, and Corrigan hesitated, wondering if he should go for his own weapon, which, in deference to the sensibilities of the governor, was snapped this day inside a holster at his ankle. To reach it would have meant having to stop, though, to spend a precious second or two, and Corrigan saw now that the governor had indeed finished up with whatever he'd come to lay on his adoring public and was making his way through a pack of back-slapping, high-fiving admirers up there on stage, his personal security occupied with fending off the crush.

The tall guy—smudge man, Corrigan found himself thinking—must finally have noticed Corrigan's approach. His awkward gait shifted, and he turned, squaring himself, bringing his raised arm down . . . just as Corrigan left his feet, driving his shoulder into the guy's midsection, sending them both to the ground, the perfect open-field tackle. Not much weight there, not much resistance at all, Corrigan thought, almost like taking down a shadow . . .

But as they tumbled, Corrigan felt his chin crack painfully off the man's knee, felt those bony legs twisting from his grasp.

They must have finally noticed something up on stage, Corrigan thought. He heard shouts of alarm from that quarter, felt someone collide with him from behind, saw Montcrief, his feet taken out from under him, crashing heavily into the risers beneath the corner of the platform.

Corrigan rolled to his feet in time to see the tall man already running away, vaulting over the rock wall that bounded the park, his long coattails flapping in his wake.

Corrigan glanced at Montcrief, who stirred groggily amid the steel supports, then at the pandemonium that had erupted on the stage itself: handlers diving for cover; the governor going down beneath a crush of bodies, some intending to protect the man, others just trying to save their own asses, Corrigan supposed.

But by this time he was up on his feet and off after smudge man. A dozen strides to the wall, up and over himself, in time to see those flapping coattails disappearing down the subway entrance. Several passersby gaped as Corrigan raced across the broad sidewalk, shouting: "Police officer! Stop!" his lungs already burning with effort.

He caught the top rail of the entrance, turned himself around, soared, hit the stairwell a dozen steps down, on the first landing. He slid across the gritty surface and banged off the wall, hearing the sound of rasping footsteps rising from the dim tunnel below.

He steadied himself, then was down the rest of the steps two and three at a time, his legs starting to go rubbery, as much from the adrenaline as fatigue. He hit the bottom at full speed, had to jump over a panhandler sitting there—a guy on a blanket spread out so you couldn't avoid him coming or going, one trouser leg pinned up, and a violin—a frigging *violin*—tucked up under his chin, the other holding a bow suspended in amazement as Corrigan flew past.

He caught sight of a couple of Transit cops and a supervisor chatting idly at the far end of the platform, down where Dawson's gleaming train idled at the ready. No sign of smudge man in that direction.

He spun about, surveyed the other end of the platform, saw a heavy-set woman with a pair of shopping bags hustling his way, glancing nervously over her shoulder. There was nothing visible behind her but a series of support pillars marching away toward the dark mouth of the tunnel, but Corrigan figured that's where the man had to be.

He felt a vague stirring in the ozone-laden air, felt the rumble, pre-sonic, growing beneath his feet, knew an uptown train was on its way. The woman, who'd probably been waiting for it, passed by him quickly, shaking her head before he had a chance to say a thing.

"No se," she mumbled bitterly as she hurried away. *"¡No se! ¡No se!"*

Corrigan started forward, moving cautiously, now, aware that his mouth had gone dry. He remembered his pistol, then—earth to Corrigan—and might have been about to go for it, when the man stepped out from behind one of the massive supports.

It could have been only an instant that they stood frozen, their stares locked, but to Corrigan it seemed to last forever. There probably had been color and detail in the clothes the guy was wearing, but those had long ago disappeared. Even his eyes were hard to make out: the pupils wide, the irises indistinct, the sclera the dusky red of old, old blood. Hard to tell where the dark fabric of his coat left off and his skin began. But one thing was clear: There was no weapon in his hands.

"Take it easy," Corrigan said, feeling himself being gauged.

That was one of the things about tunnel rats, he thought, certain of whom he was dealing with, now. They developed a supersensitivity to the nuances of the life forms around them: hostility, docility, insanity, who might hurt you, who you could scam. How else could you survive down here?

The guy's gaze sharpened, his tongue flickered, moistened his cracked lips. "We don't need more trouble," Corrigan said, trying to sound reassuring.

The guy began to back away, his eyes widening.

Corrigan felt the press of ozone-laden air from the opposite direction, knew the train was about to burst free of the tunnel. The man had begun to make wheezing sounds, as if he were having a hard time breathing.

"Just hold it, now. Hold it right there," Corrigan said, struggling for the right tone. If it wasn't commanding enough, he would lose this one, for sure. Then again, come on too strong and he'd send him flying off again.

The man was gasping, now. Instead of answering, he turned away, suddenly broke into a run.

"Goddamnit," Corrigan called. "Stop . . ."

The man glanced back, panic in his face, but he wasn't about to stop. He'd jammed his hand back into his pocket, seemed to be struggling for something.

The arriving train burst from the uptown tunnel. Corrigan hesitated, then charged. He had almost reached the man when it happened.

The man's foot caught something—a rift in the pavement, possibly, or maybe even the corrugations on the plastic safety line. He stumbled sideways, wavered for an instant, then toppled.

Corrigan lunged for him, felt his hand brush down the sleeve of the man's flapping coat, felt the leathery skin of the man's palm against his. He clutched frantically, but it was like trying to catch hold of a dream figure, like trying to gather smoke in his hands. In the next moment, Corrigan lost his grip altogether, and the man fell over with a cry.

Corrigan's mouth had opened with a shout of his own when he saw the man's body slam against the train, midair. He felt as much as heard the impact. He threw his arm up against the hail that enveloped him.

In the instant his eyes were shut, he saw his father once again, his old man glancing up as Corrigan came through the doorway into the kitchen of his parents' place in Brooklyn, drawn by who knows what premonition.

Barely two months before, it had been the same evening of the same day they'd buried his mother, the last well-wisher gone home, time to have a heart-to-heart. His father, six months retired, sat at the Formica table, a bottle of Bushmills close by, a jelly jar for a glass, nothing left in either.

His father had his service revolver out and cocked, had his mouth open and the barrel upraised, like maybe he wanted to pick something out of his teeth with a blue cylinder of steel, and who was Corrigan to interrupt?

"Dad," Corrigan said—all he could think of, all he had time to say—before his father—that sad-eyed, mournful gaze—finished the gesture, the hammer slammed down, and wetness was everywhere, a wave that blew over him like the force field of a subway express roaring through a station.

When Corrigan opened his eyes, when he could see again, the platform about him had been transformed into a scene from a charnel house.

The doors of the train hissed open. Corrigan stood transfixed, gaping dumbly inside the car. If his own father had been there, sprawled dead across a puke-green table, he would not have been surprised.

But it was not his father, of course. Just one elderly black woman alone on a bench, a thin woman in a dark blue suit, and a pillbox hat with a veil. The car's sole passenger. She sat with a twine-wrapped box between her legs, staring out at him as if she were viewing the most normal sight in the world.

His face was wet, his chest soaked. Something warm dripped from his chin.

The woman's expression did not flicker. She stared at him quietly, without surprise, without judgment. And then, as the alarm began to sound, she gathered her things and strode out across the awful platform, a person on her way toward some piece of business, passing him without a word.

CHAPTER 3

"**The boys from the precinct** are on their way, Richie. You need to talk to me."

Corrigan, who discovered he was now seated on one of the platform benches, stared up into the eyes of Jacko Kiernan. They were kindly blue eyes, he thought, set under a fine network of worry lines that fanned out across his temples, beneath his snowy white hair. The look of a confessor, of a Santa, his father's long-time friend on the force, Saint Jacko.

"I told you already," Corrigan said, wiping himself with the towel Jacko had placed in his hands. He checked himself as best he could: There was still a bit of blood on his pants, but he'd pulled off his sweater, which had taken the worst of it. He wiped his face and hands again. The awful part was over, he told himself. But his head was leaden, his thoughts bleary, disconnected.

"I know what you told me," Jacko said, looking around. "But it'd be better if you'd seen a weapon."

Corrigan shook his head. "He was running, that's all. I identified myself, told him to stop. He fell." Corrigan rubbed at his face until his skin was fiery.

Jacko nodded, glancing about the platform. The stairwells had already been blocked, and a technician was stringing yellow crime-scene tape from support girder to girder. The two trains had shut down, their silent, lightless presence as incongruous as a pair of buses left stalled in a thoroughfare.

"There's no problem with this, Richie. We just want to be sure. Get this over with quick and clean, right?"

Corrigan realized he was staring at a dark streak of blood that had dried on the back of his hand. He picked up the towel again, glanced up at Jacko as he worked, nodded.

"Look here," Jacko said.

Corrigan saw that Jacko was holding a pistol. A battered .32 caliber pistol, its butt crusted with gore, dangling from his finger by the trigger guard. Whatever had been in the black man's hand up top, it had not been this weapon, Corrigan felt sure of it.

"Where'd that come from?" Corrigan asked.

"Looks to me like it went up his windpipe and out his ass," Jacko said, glancing at the pistol.

"Don't do this," Corrigan said. "It's not necessary. I told you what happened. The driver will back me up. It was an accident."

Jacko cocked an eyebrow. "The driver didn't see shit," he said.

There was a commotion on one of the stairwells, where a pair of steel-jawed types in suits descended, a half dozen more cops in blue scuffling noisily along with them. They might have been on their way to the Yankees game, Corrigan thought.

"You want to get yourself home, get cleaned up, now, don't you?" Jacko was saying.

Corrigan nodded.

"Then just leave the fine points to me, Richie-boy," Jacko said. He clapped Corrigan on the shoulder. He moved off with a spring in his step toward the cops from the world up top.

Corrigan noticed something on the floor of the platform nearby. He bent and picked it up, holding the item between his thumb and his fore-finger. A curved piece of plastic casing, cracked, the whole of it smeared with blood.

An inhaler, he realized. About the size and shape of a derringer. Something you might shoot yourself with, *if* you had bronchitis or asthma. Corrigan glanced up.

"Jacko," he called, but the man dismissed him with a backward wave.

Jacko conferred briefly with the group at the foot of the stairs, then turned to glance at Corrigan with an odd look on his face. Jacko turned back, said something to what must have been the lead detective, then came toward Corrigan again.

"They need you up top, Richie," Jacko said. His face was a mask.

"What?" Corrigan said, feeling a fresh wave of dread. "What's happened now?"

"Just get a move on." Jacko shook his head. "It's the governor wants to see you, right away."

CHAPTER 4

"**That's him!**" Corrigan heard someone cry as he came up the last set of steps, surrounded by the knot of cops who'd come to fetch him. A sea of reporters and cameramen were gathered about the station entrance, many of whom seemed to be shouting at him, whatever they were saying lost in the sudden din.

He stared about, fighting the urge to shield his face as the cameras began to whir. Like he was a perpetrator, Corrigan thought, some hoodlum dragged up out of the underworld to face the music.

"This way," one of the plainclothesmen said, taking his arm. They shoved their way through the clamor, Corrigan's head swiveling this way and that. He caught sight of Jacko struggling after him near the back of the pack.

"Were there shots fired?" one reporter bellowed, thrusting his microphone at Corrigan like a blunted sword.

"Fuck off," the man propelling Corrigan along said, clubbing the microphone away with a swipe of his forearm.

Corrigan saw that they were heading back toward the stage where the governor had been speaking. The stage itself was empty, but there was a cluster of cops and suits gathered near the foot of the steps where Dawson had been scheduled to make his departure.

A couple of the uniformed cops stopped to lift a nylon barrier rope that had been stretched across the entrance to the park. One of them, a florid-faced guy with graying temples, gave Corrigan the look. He didn't have to say it: *Nice knowing you, asshole.*

Then Corrigan was ducking under the rope along with the plain-clothesman, leaving the reporters behind. "Worst part of the job," the burly man at his elbow said.

"You're a cop?" Corrigan asked as the din faded behind them.

"You could say that," the guy answered. Corrigan glanced ahead, saw that the gathering of cops and suits near the foot of the stage steps had parted. He saw Fielding Dawson standing there, his silver mane pressed back in place. He had his chin tilted back and seemed to be sighting down his aquiline nose at Corrigan's approach. "I'm the governor's chief of security," the guy was saying.

"Officer Corrigan." Fielding Dawson's voice boomed all about them.

Corrigan turned from the guy who'd been escorting him, back toward Dawson, dumbfounded by the sound. He stared, realizing now that Dawson was holding a microphone as he strode forward from the pack gathered by the stage. He came at Corrigan like a talk show host on location, microphone in one hand, thrusting out the other in hearty welcome.

"I want to be the first to thank the man who has saved my life." The words echoed all about them.

Still dazed, Corrigan started his own hand forward in reflex. He realized then that he still held the plastic inhaler casing he'd picked up from the grimy floor of the subway platform below.

He had a sudden flash of smudge man, then: just one more poor, addled bastard backpedaling from the law, his mouth popping like a fish's as he went in front of the train. He saw his father slumped across the kitchen table of his boyhood home, the back of his head gaping open like a passage to hell.

"Officer Richard Corrigan," Dawson's voice boomed over the still-thronged meadow. "One of New York City's finest."

"Not exactly," Corrigan heard himself saying.

But his words were lost in the cheers that arose. And he felt—as he extended his own hand toward the governor's well-tanned paw—the plastic casing that might have been a pistol go tumbling to the ground.

CHAPTER
5

NEAR BLACK MOUNTAIN, WYOMING

"**Rather slow for a holiday,** isn't it?" Bright asked the man behind the counter.

The man, clearly Native American, was resting his backside against an ancient Coca-Cola cooler. "We're off the beaten track," he said.

Bright nodded, looked again at the thing in his hand. "What is this, anyway?"

The man glanced at Bright, then at the dusky object he held. "Chip," the man said.

It was a dusty, cavernous place that seemed to swallow sound as well as light, and at first Bright thought the man had misunderstood the question, that he might have been offering his name.

Could it be? A creature out of a Frederic Remington painting with a name like Chip?

There was a black-and-white television on the counter, offering a wavy picture of a baseball game. The Indian had turned the sound down when Bright entered the store. WILD WEST SOUVENIERS, the sign outside promised. FLOTSAM AND JETSAM would have been more appropriate,

Bright thought, surveying the junk arrayed on flimsy card tables, discarded cable spools, a pair of battered picnic tables.

"Chip of what?" Bright said, though it was beginning to dawn on him.

"Buffalo chip," the man said.

Bright stared at the thing in his hands. Dull brown, hard, almost weightless, with an odd, burnished quality that gave it the appearance of having been machined. So, he was holding a piece of buffalo shit. He tossed it back into the cardboard box, along with what looked to be a hundred others that had come from the same elemental stamping press.

"People pay you five dollars for a piece of shit?"

The Indian's expression did not waver. "Some people do."

Bright nodded. "I like the profit margin."

The Indian's attention had drifted back to the television set. There might have been a batter crouched at the plate, waiting for a pitch, but then again it could have been a samurai lurking in a snowstorm, waiting to strike.

"Follow the herd around, pick up five-dollar bills right off the ground," Bright said.

The Indian turned to him. "Haven't you heard? The buffalo's all gone. White eyes killed 'em. Every last one."

Bright found himself smiling. "So, we're talking *antique* shit, then."

"What we're talking about is buffalo chips," the Indian said. "Five dollars apiece."

Bright nodded, picked up the chunk he'd been holding. Something in the notion appealed to him. He peeled a ten off the folded wad in his pocket and put it on the counter by the television. There was a commercial on now, or so he thought, perhaps a ghostly image of a woman in a tight sheath dress with her hand on the flank of an automobile. Or perhaps it was nothing, just imaginary patterns in a constantly whirling mass of snow. They were hundreds of miles from any city, and there didn't seem to be a cable attached to the set. Perhaps the Indian only *believed* he was watching television.

"You have any drinks in that cooler?"

The Indian glanced down over his shoulder as if he had just realized where he was sitting. "Coke, Sprite, Diet Coke, Yoo-Hoo," the Indian said. "Dollar each."

"Yoo-Hoo?" Bright asked, letting the question linger.

The Indian regarded him. "You *look* like a white man," he said. "But I'm guessing you could be something else."

Bright nodded. A few hours before, he'd killed four men who'd considered themselves experts in matters of violence. He suspected the one standing before him could have handled the job just as easily and probably wouldn't have lost his pants in the process. You met your equals in the most unlikely places, he thought. Next time he got to pick a partner, maybe he'd come back and talk to this man.

"Coke, then," Bright said.

The Indian shoved himself off the cooler, reached inside without seeming to look, and pulled out a dripping bottle. He handed it to Bright, flicking the cap off with his thumb as easily as if he'd used an opener.

"Ted Turner," the Indian said, nodding at the snowy television. Bright glanced over, saw nothing but an electronic blizzard. "You ever notice how much he looks like Custer?"

"No," Bright said. "Who does he play for?"

"He sits in the stands," the Indian said. "But someday he's going to make a mistake, take a trip out West."

"You think he'll come in here?" Bright said, taking a swallow of his drink.

The Indian nodded. "It's destiny," he said, and the two shared a smile.

Bright nodded, waiting as the Indian counted out his change. Bright picked up a quarter. "The sign out front says you have a pay phone."

The Indian nodded, and used his chin to point over Bright's shoulder. Bright started off.

"It's thirty-five cents, now," the Indian called.

Bright stopped, came back to the bar, found a dime among the coins. "Ted Turner's fault," the Indian said, then turned back to his game.

"It sounds as if you're on a cellular," Bright said as the connection was made.

"Don't worry," the voice on the other end assured him. "It's encrypted."

"Why should I worry?" Bright said.

"There's a reason you called, I'm certain of it."

"What's your take on buffalo chips?" Bright said. There was silence on the other end.

"You must be using code left over from some other assignment," the voice said finally.

"There's a killing to be made out here," Bright said.

"I certainly hope so," the voice replied.

Bright glanced over his shoulder at the counter. The Indian was gone, the television dark. Outside, the light seemed to be fading.

"This is to inform the client," he said. "Everything's in place."

"It is understood," the voice replied.

"You won't be hearing from me again," Bright said. "If there's anything to say, say it now."

"Have you made that other contact yet?"

"Very soon, now," Bright replied.

"You'll proceed as planned, then," the voice said. "And good luck."

"Luck doesn't enter into it," Bright said, and the connection broke.

———

Outside, he found that the sun had indeed sunk behind a distant, ragged ridgeline. A fiery band of red split the horizon: darkness below, pale blue sky above, as much sky as he'd ever seen. One star up there, or maybe a planet, given the brightness; from time to time, he regretted his lack of knowledge of the heavens, but practicalities dictated where his expertise must lie.

He scanned the parking lot, the nearby sentinel pines, but found no sign of the Indian. No car, no apparent trail, no shadow of a departing shapeshifter. There was a battered aluminum mobile home at the far edge of the lot, but something in its aspect suggested that no one had lived there for years.

If he wanted, he could walk back inside, fill his pockets full of antique buffalo shit, help himself to all the Coke and Yoo-Hoo a man might drink, carry off the quiet TV and anything else he might fancy, as well. There'd be no one to call after him, no angry shopkeeper on his tail.

He laughed at the prospect, then started toward his car. Those idiots he'd dealt with earlier in the day, they might be stupid enough to try such a thing.

Bright was in his vehicle, turning the key, about to drive off the map. He glanced off toward the great mountain that loomed in the distance. Yes, such men as those might try almost anything. And look what had happened to them.

CHAPTER 6

NEW YORK CITY

SEPTEMBER 4

"But don't you feel just a little bit ashamed of what you've done?"

This from Montel Williams to one of his guests, just as Corrigan wandered back into his cramped living room. In another life, the space had served as the common area of a two-person dorm for students at nearby Columbia Law School. His cousin Victor, then a scholarship student, now in practice in Albany, had still been in residence during the re-privatization and these days rented to Corrigan at 10 percent over his nut.

Corrigan didn't resent Victor for charging him the 10 percent. He'd sold his parents' house within a month after he'd buried his father, hadn't been back in the kitchen since the day it happened. Another consolation of death: His former hour's commute to work, with a change of trains, had shrunk to a quarter of that, one straight shot downtown.

So, everything has a bright side, Corrigan thought, glancing down at the copy of the *News* that lay on his coffee table. GUV LUVS CAVE COP—the blaring headline, a big picture of him with the governor's arm around his shoulders, the governor all teeth and gleaming hair, Corrigan looking a little bewildered, like a guy who'd been mistaken for someone else.

The story, so far as Corrigan had read into it, recounted some pretty heroic deeds. According to the writer, Corrigan not only had saved the governor from possible harm but had shielded his partner, Rollie Montcrief, from gunfire with his own body, then single-handedly pursued the would-be assassin into the bowels of the subway station, where he had overtaken the assailant and managed to wrest the man's weapon away. In the hand-to-hand struggle that had ensued, the assailant had lost his footing and fallen to his death on the tracks. While the normal departmental investigation of the incident was ongoing, blah, blah, blah . . .

Yours truly would be furloughed for a few days, now, Corrigan thought, flopping down on the musty couch Victor had left behind. And he would be free to watch as much daytime television as a man might stomach. Just now, for example, he'd been to the bathroom, then wandered to the kitchen for a fresh beer, and had come back to discover he'd missed the end of *Springer,* which had somehow morphed into the opening of *Montel.*

The kid Montel was talking to wouldn't raise his chin off his chest. He looked to be in his early twenties, a few years younger than Corrigan. On the chair next to him sat a petite blonde about the same age, in a tight skirt that extended about an inch below her panties, her hair chopped short, her eyes sporting too much mascara.

Corrigan wondered what the kid could have done to his partner to earn such censure from Montel. After airing the confessions of barnyard-animal humpers, where was there to go with these programs, anyway? Maybe he could get a shot on one of the shows: "Made My Day: I threw a homeless man into the path of a subway train."

He snapped off the set, leaned back into the ratty couch, had a slug of his beer. *Today is the first day of a lot of days off. Whoop-de-do.*

He reached back toward the battered coffee table where he'd had his feet propped, brushed a few scattered Chee-tos aside, and picked up the bankbook he'd tossed there. Fifteen thousand one hundred and twelve dollars, and sixteen cents. Plus whatever interest had accrued since the last entry, which was a couple of weeks before his old man had pulled the trigger, surely a tidy addition by now, he thought.

Richard and his mother were named in joint tenancy of the account, and she had never mentioned it. She might have failed in a number of bodily functions during those final months, Corrigan thought, but she hadn't lost her sense of what moral actions smelled to high heaven, that much was clear.

He hadn't been able to bring himself to visit the bank where the funds were kept, either, even though there were plenty of things he could use that his salary wouldn't quite cover, a new couch and coffee table among them.

He tossed the book back on the table, finished the beer, stood, and stretched. He walked into his stuffy bedroom, found a fresh shirt in the laundry bag he hadn't unpacked. He donned it, went to the equally stuffy bathroom, splashed water on his face, smoothed his hair. He was wondering if someone had come to replace Montel yet, when the telephone began to ring.

"Lotta people over here," the voice on the other end was saying.

"Over where?" Corrigan asked.

"Looking for *you*," the voice continued, the tone beyond aggrieved. "Reporters!"

By now, Corrigan had realized who it was. "Yeah, Mr. Blanco," he said to the man who'd bought his parents' house. Five grand down, just about enough to cover the costs, Corrigan carrying the paper on the balance. He hadn't gotten around to changing the home address on his Department records; somebody had probably leaked the information to the press.

"I work in the nights, okay? They waking me up for you. . . ."

"Listen, I'm sorry, Mr. Blanco. You didn't give them my number, did you?"

"No number," Blanco said. "I couldn't find."

"Great," Corrigan said. "Now, I want you to do me a favor. . . ."

"My wife tell them where you live," Blanco was saying. "Say, 'Get the hell out of here,' you know? She don't like."

"She gave them my address?" Corrigan said, a sinking feeling in his stomach.

"And chase them away with a broom," Blanco said. "I tell her, 'Come inside, Luisita,' but she don't like. . . ."

Corrigan heard a banging at his door, then. Some enterprising reporter already there, already past the lock that rarely worked in the foyer?

"I gotta go, Mr. Blanco. But don't give out my number, okay?"

"I'm not gonna," Blanco said. "But Luisita, she don't like. . . ."

"Good-bye, Mr. Blanco," Corrigan said.

The knock was sounding again, louder this time. He dropped the phone back into the cradle, turned to consider the alternatives. He could use the fire escape, he supposed, but somebody was probably climbing up the ladder already. On the other hand, he could just ignore the knocking, get himself another beer, go back to the couch. He was trying to calculate how long before he'd have to send out for more Chee-tos when a familiar voice sounded through the door.

"It's me, Richie-boy. Open up."

Corrigan felt himself relax. He hurried to the door and flipped off the lock, then swung it open.

"Man, am I glad . . ." he began, then broke off when he saw who was there with Jacko.

"Mind if we come in?" The blocky guy who'd yesterday called himself the governor's security chief was already moving toward the open doorway. It didn't seem exactly like a question.

Corrigan glanced at Jacko, who shrugged helplessly. "Why not?" Corrigan said, and ushered the two inside.

"**The governor wants me to go *where*?**" Corrigan said. He'd just come back into the living room with a fresh beer for himself, a glass of water for Jacko. The governor's man, who'd introduced himself simply as Soldinger, had declined Corrigan's limited choices.

Soldinger opened his palms neutrally. "The Absaroka is a wilderness area in north-central Wyoming," he said patiently. "I haven't been there myself."

Corrigan shook his head. "Why would he want me to go there?"

Soldinger closed his eyes briefly. "I suspect that's a question better suited for the governor," he said.

"It's one of these outward-bound trips for the well-heeled," Jacko Kiernan broke in. "The governor's had his own private expedition planned for some time."

Corrigan stared at him. "Is that supposed to explain something?"

"Officially, you've been added to the security detail," Soldinger said. "In reality—"

"It's a publicity stunt," Corrigan broke in.

"The governor would simply like to acknowledge your accomplishment and the fine work of the Department," Soldinger said, unfazed.

"You're on furlough, anyway," Jacko chimed in.

"This is bullshit," Corrigan said.

"Captain Zinn's already authorized your leave," Jacko added. He was staring down at the picture of Corrigan and the governor on the cover of the *News,* had spoken without glancing up.

Corrigan started to say something, then paused.

"Kid takes a good picture, don't he?" Jacko said to Soldinger in the awkward silence.

Soldinger shrugged.

"You mean Zinn *wants* me to do this," Corrigan said to Jacko, finally.

"It redounds to the image of his operations," Soldinger said.

"You've been bucking for a transfer, Richie," Jacko said, finally meeting his gaze. "This can't hurt a thing."

Corrigan stared back at him for a moment, holding himself in. Then he turned to Soldinger. "I don't know squat about the wilderness. I wouldn't know a bear if it bit me in the ass."

Soldinger waved his hand. "The outfitters are in charge of the trip itself. They pitch the tents, cook the food, paddle the rafts."

"Rafts?"

"I've got a list of some personal items you'll need to pick up," Soldinger said, glancing at Jacko as he reached into his coat and withdrew a folded sheet of paper.

"I'll help you out with that," Jacko added. "The Department's picking up expenses."

"You have got to be kidding me," Corrigan said.

"I'd be sure I got myself a comfortable pair of hiking boots," Soldinger said, standing up. "You may not have to do too much, but you will have to handle your own walking, as I understand."

Jacko nodded. "First rule of the cop business," he said, taking a quick swig of water as he stood along with Soldinger. "Gotta love your shoes."

Corrigan stared back, was still trying to figure if there was some translation of "No!" the two of them might understand, when the buzzer from the foyer began to ring.

"You expecting someone?" Jacko asked.

Corrigan sighed. "No one I care to see," he said wearily. He turned to Soldinger. "So, when's this trip supposed to happen?"

"There'll be a car here to pick you up first thing in the morning. The governor's plane leaves La Guardia at ten A.M."

Corrigan nodded, the buzzer an uninterrupted whine. "You might have to get me out of here, get me someplace else," he said, glancing at Jacko, who nodded his assurances.

"Whatever," Soldinger said.

"Me and Jacko," Corrigan said, "we'll just go out the back, if you don't mind. Maybe you can talk to the people down there in the foyer."

"I'll take care of it," Soldinger said.

"Yeah," Corrigan said. "I know you will."

And he followed Jacko Kiernan out.

CHAPTER 7

ELK RIVER PASS, WYOMING

"You're no cowboy, are you?"

The voice was authoritative, though not accusatory. Bright turned to regard the woman who had taken a stool at the bar beside him. She wore her dark hair in braids wrapped tightly at her ears, something that a nineteenth-century schoolmarm might have affected.

But this was otherwise no schoolmarm. The crimson blouse opened an extra button, form-fitting jeans, a pair of ostrich-skin boots, by Lucchese, perhaps. She ran her tongue over her lips, adding a bit of gloss to flesh that had been glossy enough already.

Bright thought of a succession of vampire films he had seen, and decided this woman might have played in any one of them. He also decided that there would be no shortage of candidates for her attentions.

"No," he told her. "I'm not a cowboy."

She smiled and had a sip of her drink, something with a slight bluish tint swirling in a martini glass. It seemed an unlikely choice for this bar, an oversized roadside cabin filled with locals in jeans and checked shirts, most of them with bottled beer in hand.

Her eyes met his in the mirror behind the bar, and she lifted her glass in salute. "It's a Blue Glacier," she told him. "Half gin, half vodka, with a touch of blue Curaçao. The bartender at the Four Seasons in Seattle invented it."

Bright glanced about the room, then back at her. "Are you with the local Welcome Wagon?"

She arched an eyebrow at him. "I'm all alone. Something tells me you're alone. I thought we might share some laughs."

"Why not say something funny?"

She smiled. "I can do that. Would you like one of these first?" She raised her glass to him.

Bright shook his head, indicated his tomato juice. She shrugged, had a swallow of her drink, put the nearly empty glass down before her, and clasped her hands. "Here goes," she said, offering him a brief smile.

"This cowboy's sitting in a bar, you see: hat, chaps, spurs, the whole bit. A good-looking woman spots him, comes to sit beside him." A group of genuine-looking cowboys had a spirited game of pool going in a nearby corner of the bar, and she'd leaned in close over the hubbub. Bright could feel her breath warm against his neck. Right about where she might sink her teeth, he thought.

"She asks if he's a real cowboy, and the cowboy turns in surprise. He admits he probably is. He tells her he's spent his entire life on a ranch, roping cows, riding horses, mending fences." The woman tossed her hair, baring her own neck momentarily. "She seems to accept this."

The bartender came by, and the woman made a circular motion with her finger, suggesting she'd like another drink. Bright was thinking about the sound of her voice, the unusual accent, the odd formality of her speech. When the bartender had gone, the woman leaned even closer, her breasts brushing Bright's arm. He watched her through the mirror. From that angle, she seemed poised, about to strike.

"So after a bit," she continued, "the cowboy asks the woman what *she* is." The woman ran her tongue over her lips again, held her gaze steady on Bright's. "The woman tells the cowboy that she's a lesbian. She spends her entire day thinking about women. She awakens thinking of women, thinks of them when she eats, when she showers, when she watches television. In short, everything seems to make her think of women."

Her face was so close now that Bright really could not focus. It was easier to watch her through the mirror. He sensed movement, then felt her hand come to rest on his knee.

"The woman leaves the cowboy a little while after this, and a couple comes to the bar to sit where she'd been sitting. The couple study him for a moment and finally ask if he is a real cowboy. 'I always thought I was,' the cowboy tells them, 'but I just found out that I'm a lesbian.'"

Her hand, which had risen to the inside of his thigh, squeezed slightly, then left him as the bartender delivered her drink. Bright swiveled on his stool, watched her lift the nearly full glass neatly, watched her sip.

"So, what's the punch line?" he asked.

She put her drink down and regarded him quietly for a few moments. One of the pool players sent the cue ball flying wildly off the table, and she watched, unmoving, as the young man bent near her stool to retrieve it.

The young man came up with his face inches from her knees. She smiled, and the young man tipped his hat as he rose.

When the pool game had resumed, she turned back to Bright. "In my experience," she said, "a man who lacks a sense of humor turns out to be a disappointing lay."

"I just wondered what happened to the woman in your story," Bright said. "Did she come back for the cowboy? Was she waiting outside as he left? Or perhaps he went home with the charming couple who liked him for his spurs and boots."

She regarded him for a moment. "What's in that drink of yours?" she asked finally.

"V8," he said.

"Interesting," she said.

"It was invented by an Italian steamroller operator one afternoon in Siena, when a crate of vegetables fell off a truck in front of him."

"I meant your take on my joke was interesting," she said, staring off in the direction of the pool table. The cowboy who'd had his face inches from her knees a few moments before grinned back at her.

"Unusual country, don't you think?" she said thoughtfully.

"It's the wilderness," he said. "You're not supposed to feel at home here. That's the point of it."

She turned to Bright. "I feel very much at home."

He thought of the forest outside, the unbroken sweep of rugged country that ran for hundreds of miles in every direction. She had the sharp features of a cat, the gleaming teeth, the shining, hungry lips.

Perhaps she *was* at home here. Perhaps she had been spawned here, had come down from the great distant mountain to claim some necessary thing.

"Did you have a purpose in mind when you sat down here?" he asked.

"I think you know what my purpose is," she said. Her gaze held his for a moment.

"I am Nelia," she said, extending her hand. "Nelia Esteban."

"Bright," he said, extending his own. Hers was a cool grip, and a firm one. Anything caught in it alive would have pause, he thought.

"I know who you are," she said.

"I hadn't expected a woman," he replied.

"I'd been hoping for someone with a sense of humor," she said. She motioned to the bartender, stopped Bright's hand when he went for his wallet. "Let me get this."

"Why not?" he said. "At the end of the day, it's coming out of the same pocket." He finished his drink, then turned to follow her out.

At the exit, Bright found the young cowboy holding the door open for her. The young man's grin turned to something of a sneer as Bright followed after her.

"You're lucky to be alive," Bright said as he passed the young man.

The young man gave a humorless laugh. "You some kind of badass, mister?"

Bright glanced at him mildly, then at the disappearing backside of Nelia Esteban. "Not me," he told the puzzled young man. "It's *her* you ought to be worrying about."

"Towel," she gasped, twisting her hand around behind her back. She was facedown in the big bed, her other hand clutching a wad of sheeting she'd torn loose from the mattress. "What have you done with the towel?"

Outside the windows of the hotel room, it was storming. A bolt of lightning haloed the drapes in the darkness, and a peal of thunder splintered the skies, rattling the walls of the room. He groped about with one hand, found the towel, managed to place it in her hand. The motion seemed to take the last of his energy.

He let his head roll over, glanced at her, at the vague shadow of her long black hair, unloosed from the braids, now, fanned out across the dim white glow of her flesh.

"A nice touch, those braids," he said as the sounds of the thunder faded. "Very Hester Prynne."

"Gwyneth Paltrow, actually," she said. The air-conditioning had kicked on, and a band of light from a vapor light outside leaked past a gap in the curtains. She raised herself up on one elbow, tucked the towel deftly beneath her. "Just like her hairdo at Cannes. I'm not familiar with the other actress."

Bright nodded. Perhaps she was putting him on. There was no way to know with Nelia.

"That cowboy getup you were wearing," she said. "Was it *High Noon* inspired you?"

"When in Rome . . ." he said.

"I very nearly missed spotting you," she said. "Imagine."

"I can't," he said. "I can't imagine you missing anything."

"Then I saw you at the bar, and I thought, Of course, he thinks he's in *The Wild Bunch* this go-round."

"Those films are from before your time," he said, ignoring her jab.

"Not in my country, *señor*," she mimicked. "There they are *steel* first run."

A fresh gust of wind swept over the hotel, splattering rain against the wooden siding. Another, more distant peal of thunder sounded, but the storm seemed headed away.

"Pehaps next time we should pretend we're in *Casablanca*," he said, thinking of his own favorites. "Or perhaps *The Maltese Falcon*."

"Not bloody likely," she said, mocking his own accent. "Morocco, San Francisco"—her tone was dismissive—"*this* is the only place in the world where life still looks like a movie set."

True enough, he supposed, but he didn't feel like saying so. "Or possibly we could just meet like ordinary people," he said. "Hello. How are you. Good to see you again. A peck on either cheek before bedding down."

"Who have you dispatched lately?" she chimed in. "Care to have a look at my new garrote? We're hardly ordinary people, Bright."

He nodded, grudgingly amused, but his mind had drifted to the dilemma presented to the great Bogart late in the film, where he'd played a detective who had realized he'd been sleeping with a killer. The writing had been particularly true in that regard, Bright thought. The issue was not that she had killed. If anything, that had only inflamed Bogart's passions further. It was just that she had killed his partner. There was where the moral issue lay.

"I *can* count on you," he said at last, his words floating up toward the invisible ceiling.

This made three times that they had worked together. The first time they'd met in Brunei, where he'd mistaken her for one of the Sultan's coterie, and she had played along, just to see his surprise when they were sent off to do the necessary work together. The second assignment in London, he'd been idling in Harrods, no idea who he'd be working with. He'd decided to have himself fitted for a suit, saw the salesperson going out, found her there suddenly in the dressing room playing tailor, brandishing a tape measure, her smile around a mouthful of pins.

"So long as we're employed by the same side," she said, breaking into his thoughts. Her hand had snaked its way to him, gave an affectionate squeeze.

"Tomorrow's a busy day," he said.

"How long since we've been together?" she said, dismissing him. "Tonight's a busy night."

"I'm already thinking how much there is to be done."

"Be quiet," she said, sliding closer. "You could be fucking some ordinary person. Where's the fun in that?"

"I wouldn't be fooling around at all," he said. "Not at a time like this."

"You sound like a football coach: 'Save it for the big game, men.'" Her leg swung over his.

"Normal people next time," he said. His mind was drifting, despite himself. "That's how we should be."

"Like *Last Tango in Paris,* then?"

"I'm afraid I missed that one." He was biting his lip. "I'm not much for dance."

"Oh, don't worry," she said as she turned atop him. "This is a step you're going to love."

CHAPTER 8

"You got everything you need, Richie-boy?" Jacko Kiernan didn't seem too concerned about the answer. He had his mug of coffee in his hands and was staring out the café window at a woman in leopard-skin pants standing near the curb as if she were waiting to hail a cab. He turned back to Corrigan as a sedan pulled up, and the woman slid smoothly inside.

"I'm fine," Corrigan said. As it had turned out, the list Soldinger had provided him stipulated more of what would be provided for him than what he would need to bring. No tent, no sleeping bag, no backpack, no serious equipment necessary.

He'd been told to show up in uniform for the big sendoff, but after that, he was free to wear whatever he chose. Practical enough, Corrigan supposed, but just one more sign this was all for the sake of public relations. He'd picked up some jeans, some extra socks, a couple of sweatshirts, a light parka made of something called Gore-Tex, all of it stashed with his toiletries in a nylon bag there on the seat beside him.

They were sitting in a place not far off the Grand Central Parkway. Go one way, you'd be on your way out to Rikers. Just to the east was La

Guardia. He'd been in the café with his old man a couple of times. Tom Corrigan, he thought. Never missed a spot where a cop could get a cup on the cuff.

"You get that pair of hiking boots?"

Corrigan stretched his leg out from beneath the table between them. Jacko glanced down.

"Those are tennis shoes."

Corrigan shrugged. When the clerk at Outdoor World had opened the box, revealing the mesh uppers, the stitched Nike swoosh, Corrigan had said the same thing. "The kid told me these were the latest thing in boots. *Très* hip."

"Tray, my ass," Jacko said. "You want a pair of shoes you can kick something when you have to."

Corrigan nodded, glancing at his watch. "Sounds like something my old man would have said." He noted that the sedan outside hadn't pulled away, but the woman's head had disappeared. Jacko had his chin raised toward the café window as if he were trying to get a look inside the car.

"It was, in fact," Jacko said, still staring out the window. "I always liked the line. Now it's mine." He gave Corrigan a smile.

Corrigan reached into his shirt pocket and tossed the bankbook down on the table between them.

"What's that?" Jacko asked.

"Take a look," Corrigan said.

Jacko opened it, flipped the pages. He folded it closed, slid it back across the table to Corrigan. "Your father was a thrifty man," he said.

"My mother never mentioned this money," Corrigan said.

Jacko shrugged. "She was in a lot of pain there at the end. She was taking a lot of pills."

Corrigan shook his head. "The doctor bills had been mounting up a long time before that, Jacko. She could have used that money. But she wouldn't."

The waitress came by to refill their coffee, and Jacko waited until she was gone to reply. "What do you want from me, Richie?"

"I spent all of a half hour with Internal Affairs yesterday," Corrigan said. "They couldn't have cared less about that poor bastard who died. They don't even know his name," he said with a significant pause. "But they sure as hell had to know where that gun came from. . . ."

"On my soul, it was right there on the platform. . . ." Jacko said, lifting his right hand.

"Can it, Jacko. You wanted to take care of me, the Department's just happy to avoid a black eye. I'm the one keeps getting to see the guy's face going over the side."

Corrigan paused, and glanced down at the table. "The other thing I thought about was this." He tapped the bankbook with his finger.

Jacko glanced briefly at the bankbook. "I'm not with you, son."

"Just tell me, Jacko. How'd he get the money? Who'd he squeeze? Who was he shaking down?"

"You're making a lot of assumptions over fifteen thousand dollars, boy-o. If your father had been crooked, he'd have come away with a lot more than that."

"My old man never thought big," Corrigan said. "I'd just like to know how he came by it. Just what scams he could stomach. We didn't get much of a chance to talk there at the end, you know."

The woman in the leopard pants was out of the car already, blotting her lipstick with a handkerchief as the sedan pulled away. "I remember when I could go as quick as that," Jacko said, turning to Corrigan with a wistful smile.

He saw the expression on Corrigan's face and broke off. He put his palms on the table, leaned forward. "That was a terrible thing you had to go through, Richie. A terrible thing. But it had nothing to do with you. And your old man was no crook. He was a stand-up guy who didn't know what to do with himself once he was out of harness. When your mother died, that must have finished him."

"He still had a son," Corrigan said.

Jacko stopped, drew a deep breath. "He thought the world of you, Richie."

"It must have killed him, me stuck in the caves."

Jacko shook his head. "He was proud of you. He felt as bad as anybody about . . ." Jacko paused, searching for words. "About you getting hurt."

Corrigan nodded, and felt his hand go unconsciously to his eye. "He never said anything about that, either."

Jacko studied him for a moment, then finally clasped his hands together. "Your old man had his problems, Richie, but what's past is past. You got to take advantage of what's laid in front of you. You go off on this trip, go someplace where you can breathe fresh air, get your head cleared out, know what I mean? By the time you come back, you'll feel a lot better. I wouldn't be surprised to see that transfer waiting for you."

Corrigan stared at him. "Everything swept under the rug, I put on the blue, wait my turn to blow my own brains out? Maybe I'm barking up the wrong tree, Jacko. Maybe I ought to explore another line of work."

Jacko stared at him. "Aye, but you're a tough case," Jacko said, his descent into brogue only underscoring how deeply he felt. As a child, Corrigan had been able to gauge just how drunk Jacko and his father had become, just how close to some dream of Ireland they had drifted, by the same measuring stick.

"Just take this opportunity, son."

"Go wander in the wilderness with Dawson, we can sort out our lives together?"

"You deserve some pleasure in life."

Corrigan sat back in the booth, too weary to continue. He pocketed the bankbook and stood, tossing some bills on the table. "Thanks for the heart-to-heart, Jacko. It was life-altering. And thanks for everything, okay? Trying to keep me out of trouble, putting me up last night, keeping the reporters away . . ."

"Richie-boy . . ."

The woman in the leopard pants had turned full-face toward the window of the café and was running her tongue about her glistening lips. Just checking her reflection, Corrigan told himself, but it seemed her gaze was burning into his. You take the hand that's dealt you, that look seemed to say. You take the hand that's dealt you.

"Let's just go to the airport," Corrigan said. "Like you say, I need a change of scene."

CHAPTER 9

"I want to reassure the people of New York that the commitment of my administration to the welfare of this great state continues undiminished," Fielding Dawson said as flashes popped and cameramen jockeyed for position in the claustrophobic section of the departure lounge set aside for the press conference.

Corrigan, who'd been delivered to the proper concourse only moments before by Jacko, stood off to one side of the podium, part of a coterie that included Soldinger and a burly-looking type in plainclothes who looked like he'd spent far too much time at the steroid bar.

Dawson, who was clad in a sport coat and a checked shirt without a tie, looked uncomfortable in the getup, like some judge who wasn't quite sure how to act when he wasn't behind the bench. But the guy had undeniably rugged good looks and kept himself in careful shape, Corrigan had to admit. It was probably an image that would play well in the heartland.

"My wife, Elizabeth, and I have been planning this trip for more than a year. Despite all the talk that's going around, nothing has changed in the Dawson camp. We'll spend a few days in the wilderness doing some considerable soul-searching . . ." Here he broke off, while the cameras turned for a wave from his wife. "And then we will make our decision known.

"Until then . . ." he added, raising his hands in apparent benediction, "I am the governor of the greatest state on earth, and I am very proud of it." A cheer arose from a group of supporters near the front of the room, with one heavyset man leading a chorus of wuffing that quickly died out.

"Now, one more thing before we go . . ." Dawson was saying. Corrigan wasn't paying much attention. He'd been scanning the crowd, noting Jacko's encouraging visage toward the back, idly assessing the pert figure of a young female reporter near the front of the crowd. Unlike most of her more formally attired peers, she was dressed in jeans and flannel shirt; instead of jostling with the rest of the mob, shouting out questions that tended to blur into one unintelligible roar, she kept her head bent, scribbling continually on a pad she carried. He particularly liked the way she paused to lick the tip of her pencil from time to time. It was a trait of his mother's, he realized abruptly. Dawson's voice reduced to a background drone in his mind. A somehow endearing piece of business he'd forgotten until now.

She glanced up suddenly, her gaze locking on his, and Corrigan quickly looked away, feeling his cheeks begin to burn.

". . . so you can understand why I am not about to venture into such uncharted territory without him, one of this city's finest, Officer Richard Corrigan."

Corrigan blinked as a wave of applause came from the crowd, accompanied by a fresh round of wuffing from the man who was assuredly a member of the Dawson camp. It had dawned on Corrigan by now what he'd just tuned out of in Dawson's speech, why the girl's glance had been drawn to his.

Dawson had turned to him, with his hand extended. "These people have been dying to hear from you, Officer. Come on up and say a few words."

Corrigan stood transfixed, staring at Dawson. The man held his megawatt smile intact as Corrigan hesitated, but there was a sinister edge in his eyes, it seemed. Corrigan felt a nudge at his back, Soldinger's big paw shoving him forward. He glanced out at the crowd again, saw Jacko's beaming face, his spirited thumbs-up. The young reporter he'd had his eye on a moment before had left off with her note-taking and was regarding him with interest.

Already there were shouts from the others, a cacophony of questions that clearly would only grow. Corrigan took a deep breath and felt his feet carrying him toward the podium as the flashes popped anew.

He leaned toward the microphones clipped there, cleared his throat, stepped back as a squeal of feedback sounded. "I just wanted to clarify that I'm a member of the Transit Authority Police," he said. He glanced around nervously, seeing nothing, now. "So I don't get out much. . . ." There was a wave of appreciative laughter.

"Did you think you were going to die?" someone bellowed from the pack.

Corrigan hesitated, turned to the governor, whose posture seemed to be urging him on: *Hell, yes, man. Braved a hail of bullets, dodged a fusillade of fire.*

He turned back to the podium, then, leaned close to the bank of microphones. "I was just doing my job," he found himself saying. "There's really nothing more to it than that."

He stepped back, and though Dawson had to have been disappointed, he was quick to jump in. "A typical selfless statement from a true hero, ladies and gentlemen. Let's hear it again for Officer Richard Corrigan."

There was a fresh burst of applause, but Corrigan wasn't really aware of it. Somehow, he managed to make it back to his place by Soldinger, where he stood with his face flaming, his eyes fixed firmly on the floor.

After a few moments, Corrigan realized that Dawson had uttered some wrap-it-up farewell, and he allowed himself a glance toward the podium. The attention had shifted back to where it had been, of course: The governor had turned to embrace his wife, ignoring the reporters crying out for any scrap of confirmation that he had in fact decided to seek his party's nomination for the presidency.

"Leander Polk says he's stepping aside for you, Governor," a network correspondent with a particularly commanding voice called.

Dawson turned for that one. "Last month, Leander Polk wanted Colin Powell to be his running mate," he said. "I wouldn't put much stock in these rumors."

The correspondent tried to get in a follow-up, but he was drowned out by his colleagues, who were advancing on the Dawsons like lepers toward the gates of Lourdes.

"Let's get him out of here before they eat him," Soldinger grumbled to the steroid abuser at Corrigan's shoulder, and then they all were being hustled toward the doors.

CHAPTER 10

Corrigan, who had a row to himself, had been leaning against the blurry window, nearly lulled to sleep by the unending roar of the big plane's engines. He'd been halfheartedly trying to calculate how much of the continent they'd covered, but with the ground obliterated now by a screen of clouds, he'd been reduced to the grossest level of guesswork.

He'd flown to Chicago once to visit his cousin Victor and his family, the summer after his eye had been injured, and he'd spent the whole trip out and back trying to trace the features of the landscape below, somehow imagining that he'd be able to distinguish one state and region from the other in the same way he'd been able to in his school atlas—he'd probably expected dotted lines and squiggly topographical features. It had been quite a disappointment when he'd discovered the truth, he recalled, staring down at the vague landscape below him, now.

"Mind if I talk to you?"

He glanced up, bleary-eyed, doing a double-take when he found the reporter he'd had his gaze on at the press conference staring down at him.

"My name's Dara Wylie," she said, smiling, extending her hand. "I work for *USA Magazine.* I did a piece a few months ago about the mayor's efforts to upgrade the image of the subways . . . ?"

Corrigan had no idea what story she was talking about. But he did find her even more attractive at this close distance, and was trying not to gawk. She had straight sandy hair cut just above the shoulders, no makeup that he could perceive, and a pair of guileless hazel eyes that regarded him carefully, seeming to take his measure. He saw a spray of freckles across the V of flesh at her open collar, and forced his gaze not to drift toward her breasts.

Did he mind if she talked to him? *Careful, Richie-boy. Careful.*

"I can't really go into what happened," he told her. "The matter's still under investigation."

"I understand," she said. "I wouldn't ask you anything uncomfortable. Just a couple of questions about your part in all this." She waved her hand toward the front of the plane, where Dawson and his immediate party were sequestered in the first-class cabin.

"You just said you wouldn't ask anything uncomfortable," Corrigan told her.

She turned back to him, puzzled.

He smiled. "Just a dumb joke," he said. "The truth is, I'm more or less along for the ride, that's all."

She was staring at him uncertainly.

Duh, Richie. Don't let her get away. Tell her anything. Your shoe size. Your freaking middle name.

"You're welcome to sit down," he said. "Please."

She glanced over her shoulder, then settled into the seat on the aisle. She leaned out and seemed to signal to someone farther up in the plane. She turned back to him, gave him an apologetic smile. "I'm supposed to have a few minutes with the governor," she said. "You know how it is. I may have to get up and run."

"Sure," he said. "Whatever."

"Well," she said. "This must be pretty exciting for you." She glanced at him again. "Or maybe not. What you just said, I mean."

He saw that she hadn't opened her notebook. "It's something, all right."

"But uncomfortable."

"You could say that."

"Because you feel like the governor's show pony."

"Excuse me?" He turned to stare at her.

She dropped her eyes. "I'm sorry," she said. "I shouldn't have said that." She came back with an ingenuous smile. "You're supposed to let the interviewee do the talking."

He shrugged. "You been at this long?"

Her smile was more practiced this time. "Long enough," she said.

"Anyway, it's okay," he told her. "You more or less hit the nail on the head."

Her gaze softened. "Why don't we start over?" she said. "I'm not here to embarrass you, if that's what you think."

She glanced around, making sure there was no one else listening in. But they were well toward the rear of the sparsely populated charter. One flight attendant lounged near the service galley, flipping through a copy of *Elle;* a guy with a photographer's gear jacket zipped under his chin was stretched across the row catty-corner, apparently fast asleep.

"We do *people* pieces, okay? It's not like they send *me* to cover the war in Bosnia, you know."

"You're telling me you're doing a puff piece on the governor?"

It was her turn to shrug. She flashed her more professional smile. A good one, he thought. Give this woman a couple more years in the business, she could probably slide in beside Connie Chung, nudge her right off her chair.

"The governor is positioning himself," she said. "He's going out

West to brave the wilderness and prove to the American public that he's not just an East Coast guy with a God complex. He's going to climb mountains and bang Boy Scouts together to start fires. He's going to scare off grizzlies, catch trout, and shoot rapids, and when he comes out the other end, he's going to rhapsodize about the glories of the American experience, detail a plan to rededicate our energies to the preservation of the environment and our bedrock verities, and *then* announce his run for the presidency."

He stared at her, noting the flush that had arisen in her cheeks. Freckles there, too, he saw now, though they hadn't been visible before. He was also thinking maybe he'd been wrong a moment ago. Forget Connie Chung. This woman could boot Dan Rather out of his chair. "Sounds like a plan to me," Corrigan said.

"And I'll be there to record it, every step of the way," she said. "Seven days and seven nights in the wilderness, big press conference at the end." She nodded at the sleeping photographer across the way. "There's a film crew going along, shooting a documentary, but ours will be the first story out."

He glanced at her. "You're going on the trip?"

She studied him. "It'll make it a lot easier to write the piece," she said, her honest smile returning.

"I guess so." Corrigan nodded. Was he doomed forever to be so obvious to women? he wondered. Why not just let his tongue dangle, drool a few drops down the front of his chest? "So, you want to do a sidebar on the honorary chief of security?"

She shrugged. "You looked so miserable back there at the airport. I found myself wondering why."

"Yeah, well, maybe I'm not so good in crowds."

"Then you picked the wrong line of work, didn't you?"

He smiled. "I don't have to do a lot of talking to the people on the subway platforms," he said. " 'Keep it moving.' 'Step back.' 'No jumping the turnstiles, now.' "

She nodded, glancing up the aisle. *Not so fascinating, Richie-boy.
She still cares more about the governor than you.*

"You wanted to be a cop because of your father," she said casually.

He felt his guard raise suddenly. "You know about my dad?"

She shrugged. "Someone must have told me."

Something in her expression seemed troubled. It certainly was troubling him. He realized he'd been riding this seesaw since the moment she'd sat down next to him—salivating one instant, on his guard the next.

Things had been a lot less complicated with Angela Caravetti, sister of his boyhood pal Angelo. The last year or so—right up until his parents' deaths, anyway—they'd gone out once or twice a month: the movies, sometimes the Italian place the other side of her father's dry-cleaning shop there by Pratt Institute. Quite often they had sex, of a sort, on the couch of her parents' living room, Angela as apparently content with the arrangement as any normal, red-blooded guy not in love might hope.

But Corrigan sensed he was reaching the end of his play-it-as-it-lays rope. He was tired of feeling uncomfortable, up to his ears with holding it in. All of a sudden, he didn't care if he drove Dara Wylie away, no matter what she looked like, no matter if he ended up in her send-Fielding-Dawson-to-the-White-House magazine story as the biggest oaf in the history of fluff journalism.

"I think it's about time we cut the bullshit," he told her, his voice even.

She blinked, the color rising in her cheeks again. "I'm sorry?" she said.

"Stop with the pretense," he said. "I'm a cop, remember? Even down there in the caves, we get plenty of people running their scams. After a while, you develop a kind of radar, okay?"

There was silence for a moment. "Maybe you're a pretty good cop," she said, finally. She glanced down at her hands for a moment, seemed to make a decision. "The truth is," she said, glancing back up at him, "there is something I wanted to discuss with you—"

"Miss Wylie," a familiar voice cut in.

Corrigan glanced up and found Fielding Dawson himself standing in the aisle, his sport coat shed, the full force of his smile trained on Dara. "I'm sorry to have kept you waiting."

Dara gave Corrigan an apologetic glance. "That's all right," she said to Dawson. "You're a busy man . . . and likely to get busier."

Dawson held up his palm to stop her. "Not on this trip," he said. "That's the very point of it, to get as far from the spotlight as is possible. We'll take up the business of the campaign, assuming I decide to go ahead with it, once we've returned."

And once the public appetite has been whipped up by seven *more* days of speculation, Corrigan thought, wondering what on earth she'd been about to say. Now he'd have to wait while she took down the plan: how Candidate Dawson was to come back from wandering the wilderness after all those lonely days and nights, bearing the balm for all our aches and fears. Maybe he intended to serve fishes and loaves at the press conference, as well.

Corrigan noticed that Dawson's gaze had drifted toward his own. "Ever do much camping, Officer?"

"You don't want to know how much," Corrigan said easily.

Dawson gave a hearty laugh. "Well, the outfitters tell me we're going places the average person has never seen." He glanced briefly at Dara. "I understand you grew up in this part of the country, Ms. Wylie. Idaho, wasn't it?"

Dara glanced back at Corrigan. "Utah," she said, nodding.

"Mormons." Dawson nodded. "Salt of the earth. Nixon trusted them with his life. So did Howard Hughes."

"I'm not a Mormon, though," she said.

Dawson seemed not to hear. He stepped back slightly, made a sweeping gesture toward the first-class cabin. Dara stood and gave Corrigan a last, earnest look.

"I'm sorry, Richard," she said.

"If I'm interrupting . . . ?" Dawson said. He looked at Corrigan, making it clear he couldn't have cared less what he might have been interrupting.

"No," Corrigan said. "We were just chatting."

"We'll talk later," Dara said, moving away.

"Sure," Corrigan said.

Then Dawson had placed a proprietary hand on her shoulder and was guiding her away down the aisle.

Corrigan watched them disappear through the curtain, thinking that while he had *heard* of Utah, he'd never actually met a person who claimed to be from there. He was also considering that whatever she'd been trying to draw out of him, as a native of the West, she had yet another advantage on him.

The plane gave a sudden lurch, then, popping through an updraft that rattled the overhead bins and lightened him in his seat momentarily. There was a beeping sound from the intercom, followed by the voice of a flight attendant. "The captain has turned on the seat-belt sign in preparation for our descent into the Denver airport. Please make sure your trays and seat backs are locked and in the upright position. . . ."

The plane was jouncing steadily, now, the engines groaning as the updrafts swirled. As the plane began to bank, Corrigan caught sight of a much different landscape out the opposite windows, an unbroken sweep of brownish plain that ended abruptly in the distance, where it seemed that a great bank of thunderheads had massed.

He noted that the photographer was awake, now, and was struggling to get himself buckled into his seat belt. The guy glanced at Corrigan, who gestured out the window.

"Looks like we're in for a storm," Corrigan said, pointing.

The guy turned to look out, then gave Corrigan a quizzical look. "What do you mean?" he asked.

"Out there," Corrigan said. "All those thunderclouds at the horizon."

The photographer glanced out at the jagged blue-black mass, then back at him. "I don't know what the hell you're talking about," he said, "but those aren't thunderheads. Those are the Rocky Mountains."

CHAPTER 11

At the Denver airport, they'd been transferred to a twin-engine propeller-driven plane for what was announced as a "short" flight to Jackson, Wyoming, three hundred miles or so away. While there was no first-class cabin in the smaller plane and their party took up many more of the available seats, there would have been little opportunity for conversation above the racket of these engines, even if Dara had had it on her mind to explain herself.

He hadn't seen her or Dawson get off the jet, and though Corrigan had found a seat near the back of the smaller plane, leaving a space beside him, it did no good. When she did come on board, just ahead of Dawson and Soldinger, she settled into a spot several rows ahead and had launched into a fervent note-taking session once they were off the ground—working over some of Dawson's more pungent quotes, Corrigan supposed.

Corrigan, seated alone again, contented himself with the fact that this plane had climbed to nowhere near the altitude of the jet carrying them to Denver, and spent his time studying the landforms below. To his surprise, he found that this rugged topography *did* bear a resemblance to some of the maps he had studied as a youth. Mountain ranges stood out in clear relief, green at the lower elevations, increasingly brown and gnarled at the higher reaches. Rivers etched the land clearly, opening deep chasms through layers of red and orange and yellow rock. Roads, where there were any, were just as clearly defined.

Even to a kid whose idea of the wilderness was an unbuilt lot, this was country you could make sense of, he thought, at least from the vantage point of a growling plane.

By the time the plane neared Jackson, dusk had fallen, and though the pilot informed them that the not-to-be-missed spectacle of the Teton Range was coming up just off their port side, the combination of the failing light and gathering clouds obscured Corrigan's view. Still, even in those vague, looming shadows he saw enough to know that something amazing lay out there, some gathering of earth matter even mightier than the tons of rock that lay over his head each day of his working life back in Manhattan, and that was no puny concept in itself.

They landed at the Jackson airport without incident and were whisked by limousine (Dawson and his party) and small bus (the rest of them) to their hotel, a massive turreted and clapboard structure that looked like Teddy Roosevelt might have supervised its design and construction. A broad porch surrounded the main floor, where a series of rocking chairs had been set up, all of them filled by what seemed to be tourists in stiff jeans and colorful plaid shirts, some of them sporting cowboy hats.

He found himself assigned to a far more spacious room than he'd anticipated, with a four-poster bed sitting so high that he'd have to roll into it, and a claw-foot tub in the bath. He drew as hot a bath as he could stand, and soaked himself for an hour while leafing through a paperbound coffee-table volume he'd found on his bedside table: *High Country Visions,* a series of photographs of country so rugged and striking that Corrigan wondered if they'd been faked. It was about as dramatic an array of natural formations—snowy peaks, white-water gorges, alpine meadows—as could be imagined. Corrigan had never seen an antelope or an elk or a bear outside a zoo, and in fact suspected that such creatures truly existed only in such places. But here, if the photographic record was to be believed, the creatures abounded in the nearby territory he was about to visit.

He was no fan of Fielding Dawson, but on the other hand, the man had certain instincts for what made an arresting backdrop, no doubt about it. Corrigan dragged himself out of the tub, thinking how much more interesting commuters might find the subway if there was the chance of happening on a clutch of deer scampering up a stairwell now and then. Or imagine catching sight of the odd wolf or two, howling at the end of a lonely midtown platform late at night. Rather have that than the specter of a Brooklyn posse drag-assing toward you at 2:00 A.M., wouldn't you?

Maybe he'd make the suggestion to his superiors when he got back, he thought as he stepped happily into a pair of jeans. He was beginning to mellow, he realized. There was Dara, for one thing. And, if nothing else, he'd be out of uniform for a week, the first time in several months since he and Montcrief had been assigned a plainclothes stakeout trying to catch the heinous criminal who'd been jamming a series of turnstile coin slots with gum, then sucking the tokens out by mouth. Montcrief had been incredulous, and Corrigan might not have believed it himself, but they'd finally captured the entire process on videotape, had snagged the poor bastard in the station beneath Bloomingdale's, his lips still puckered up to one of the turnstiles. Business couldn't have been so good, anyway, with more and more people using the MetroCard instead of the tokens. The guy was a loser all the way around.

But it all seemed so far away, now, he thought as he snapped his new jeans, then reached to study the handout they'd been given by one of Dawson's aides. Dinner in something called the "Sacajawea Room" at 7:30. "Briefing" to follow.

He combed his hair, decided against a shave, then made his way down to the lobby in an elevator so ponderous, so loaded with brass, he felt as if he were riding in a safe. When he asked directions of the desk clerk to the meeting room, he didn't bother trying to pronounce "Sacajawea," and neither did the desk clerk, an affable older man wearing a shirt with pearl snaps on the pockets.

"I'm trying to find this place," Corrigan said, sliding the memo across the gleaming mahogany counter.

"Right across that way," the clerk said, pointing across the high-ceilinged lobby, "and down the hall, there."

Corrigan thanked him and walked away, thinking of how the last time he'd asked directions in the city, he'd had to flash his shield to a fellow cop to get cooperation. He skirted an outcropping of overstuffed leather sofas arranged beneath a chandelier that would have looked good in the ballroom of the *Titanic,* dodged what he saw was an actual, operating spittoon beside one armchair, noted a series of stuffed animal heads mounted on the wall beneath a railed gallery on the mezzanine.

He had stopped to stare up at the array of glassy-eyed creatures when he heard the voice over his shoulder. "Not very politically correct of them, is it?"

He glanced over his shoulder and saw Dara approaching him with a smile. Her hair was still wet from the shower, and she'd combed it straight back behind her ears. She was wearing jeans, low-cut hiking boots, and a flannel shirt with the sleeves rolled to the elbows. It was a look many of the tourists had affected. On Dara it was natural.

"You look . . . healthy," he said, searching for the right words. She looked far more than that to Corrigan, but every other phrase seemed impossible.

She looked at him. "My father might have said something like that."

Corrigan nodded. "It's a compliment," he said.

She nodded, her smile broadening at his discomfort. "I'm taking it as a compliment."

"My old man would have told you, 'If you don't have your health, you don't have anything.'"

"I'm sorry I never met your father," she said.

He stared at her. "That more or less brings us back to where we were before, doesn't it?"

She stared at him for a moment. "It does, doesn't it?"

She glanced at the open doors to the meeting room, where waiters were bustling about the seated guests. "How about I buy you a drink after dinner?"

He shook his head. "I'm a cop. We can't accept gratuities."

She smiled. "Then you can buy me one."

"You got it," he said, and followed her into the room.

CHAPTER 12

"**How come it has the head on?**" he said, leaning close to Dara. They were seated near the end of one of the two long tables that had been set up in the room, one peopled by the media types, the other by Dawson and his immediate entourage.

She glanced at him. "So you can tell it's a fish," she said mildly.

"What kind of fish?" Corrigan asked.

"Trout," she said. "That's the way we do trout out West."

Corrigan was trying to think of some response, when there was an amplified thumping from the front of the room. Corrigan turned to find that one of the rugged-looking types who had been sitting at Dawson's table was standing at a podium set up near the front of the meeting room.

The murmur of conversation in the room gradually died away, and the tall man, who, with his chiseled good looks and Western attire, could have easily posed for a Marlboro ad, continued. "I'm Ben Donnelly," he said. "I run Outback Expeditions, the outfit in charge of our little foray into the wilderness."

Donnelly nodded toward the back of the room, where an assistant, an even taller, somewhat bulkier replica of Donnelly, stood by a cart bearing a slide projector. "This is my son, Chipper," Donnelly said. "He'll be with us on the trip as well." Donnelly extended his hand toward his son. "Chipper!"

There was a polite smattering of applause as Chipper, clearly not an attention seeker, nodded a greeting. He turned to a panel on the wall and flipped a switch. The lights went down, and the slide-projector beam jumped to life.

A topographically enhanced map of the Intermountain West now filled a screen, which had been lowered just to Donnelly's side. The rendering featured every aspect of the maps Corrigan had pored over as a child, and he felt an odd thrill wash over him as he surveyed the vast sweep of mountain ranges, river courses, attendant canyons and valleys. Even the dotted lines outlining the familiar shapes of the states were there: Idaho, Montana, a chunk of northeastern Nevada, northern sections of Utah and Colorado, and, of course, Wyoming. There was a sizable red dot in the northwestern corner of the latter, and a "You Are Here"–styled arrow pointing to the spot he presumed was Jackson.

Donnelly, who had donned a pair of reading glasses, was bent to the podium, his face reflecting the glow of a reading lamp. "This is the big picture," Donnelly said, speaking with the air of a man who had been through the script before. "And it *is* a mighty big picture, folks. More beautiful, undeveloped territory here than anywhere else on earth."

He glanced out at his audience over his glasses. "That's part of the point of our journey, after all. To give you all a sense of what this country is all about."

"Hear, hear," Corrigan heard someone say. After a moment, he realized it was Dawson chiming in.

Donnelly managed a smile and gestured at his son. "Whyn't you bring 'em in a little closer to the subject, Chipper?"

There was a clunking sound as the changer cycled and another view came up on the screen, this one drawn down tighter on Wyoming. The extreme northwestern corner of the state was crosshatched off to show the boundaries of Yellowstone National Park, an assemblage of rugged peaks surrounding the vivid blue sprawl of Yellowstone Lake. The peaks weren't confined to the boundaries of the park, to be sure, and in fact, some of the country farther east, on the northern border of the state, seemed, if anything, even more rugged.

Just south of Yellowstone was another area of peaks and lakes and rivers, and there Corrigan saw the familiar dot representing Jackson. "We're *here*," Donnelly said, "and first thing in the morning we'll be flying up *here*."

As he spoke, the slide changed once more, where a yellow dotted line indicated a semicircular course into the heart of the rugged tangle well east of Yellowstone. Corrigan found himself barraged with exhilarating images of old films, with their treasure maps, newsreels tracing Lindbergh's flight to Europe, Amelia Earhart's doomed course over the Pacific. No wonder people wanted to be cartographers, he thought. Maybe that was a career he could look into. But what was the job market like for cartographers? he wondered.

The slide changed again, depicting a vast expanse of forest, glacier-strewn peaks, deep canyons, one sizable lake at the farthest reaches. "No roads where we're headed. No houses, no people, no newspapers, no cell-phone service." There were a few chuckles. "The deer and the bears don't need any of that." More chuckles, though Corrigan saw a look of concern on the face of one of the women across the table from him.

"Now, I don't want anyone to be concerned about safety. That's why we're there. Besides, those creatures don't want anything more to do with you than vice versa. We'll see some squirrels and a deer or two. But probably no bears . . . unless you ignore the basic rules concerning food storage and the like that we'll be going over with you later, of course."

Donnelly gestured again, and this time the new scene elicited a murmur from the audience. It was a ground-level shot taken from the shores of a peak-encircled lake, perhaps the same one from the previous slide.

The sky was crystal, the water cobalt. In the distance, at the head of the lake, a waterfall cascaded down a sheer rock face, a lacelike trail of white against the near-black backdrop of cliff.

"This is where we begin," Donnelly said, glancing up at them, his glasses gleaming in the reflected light. Corrigan couldn't see the man's eyes, just those glowing half-moons high up on his cheeks. Just as well, he thought. It made him seem like some kind of prophet of the wilderness. He was also beginning to understand why people would shell out whatever astronomical sum was required to take this trip.

"The first day we circle the lake, camp beside Bridal Lace Falls, there, then start through the mountains. Six days through some of the prettiest country you'll ever see, then to Garrett's Canyon, the best part of a day climbing down, and then two days on the river coming out, back to civilization." He'd said all this to a rapidly shifting panorama of rock formations, dizzying overlooks, and winding trails, capped off with a shot of a series of yellow rubber rafts hurtling through white-water rapids in a deep gorge.

Donnelly gestured again, and the lights came up. He smiled out at the blinking audience. "Of course, I didn't show you any of the best stuff," he said. "We're saving that for the trip, right, Chipper?"

Chipper colored, managing a nod for the group.

Corrigan turned to Dara. "I foresee a challenge, getting Chipper involved in your story," he said.

"If we meet any grizzlies, he's the one I want in front of me," she said.

Corrigan nodded, and turned back as a carefully groomed man at Dawson's table raised a hand. "I've heard rumors these trips are well provisioned," the man said, meaning it as a question.

"I should introduce all of you to Giles Ashmead," Dawson called, smiling out over the crowd. "As some of you know, Giles is my attorney and chief advisor. This lovely woman he's sitting with is his wife, Sonia."

The pair smiled perfunctorily, and Corrigan thought they seemed more likely to be found sitting at a society fund-raiser than at the kickoff dinner to a wilderness trip. He wondered just how eager the two of them were to be making this trek.

"You won't go hungry," Donnelly assured Ashmead. "Or thirsty," he added, to general laughter from the Dawson table.

"I was just wondering how many bearers there'll have to be," Ashmead continued.

Donnelly gave a laugh of his own. "Well, we don't use *bearers* here in Wyoming, Mr. Ashmead. We have some *wranglers* that manage our pack animals—horses and mules, that is. But they won't be with us. That would slow everything down too much. Fact of the matter, they're already up there caching what we'll need at various spots along the way. We'll just carry in a few of the basics so we can move along unencumbered."

Corrigan leaned back to Dara. "Yeah, those cases of Chateau Lafitte Rothschild get a little heavy toward the end of the day."

"I'd be happy with a Coors Lite every once in a while," she said.

Corrigan sat forward again, noticing that Dawson's wife had her hand aloft. "I know you have a lot of experience at what you do, Mr. Donnelly, but what if something *should* happen, an accident of some kind . . . ?"

Donnelly held up a reassuring hand. "I understand exactly where you're coming from, Mrs. Dawson. And while it is important to us to maintain the sense of a true wilderness experience, we have to be prepared."

He turned back to his son. "Chipper, you got your new phone with you?"

Chipper nodded, lumbering toward the front of the room like a well-trained bear himself. He handed his father something that looked much like an ordinary cell phone. Donnelly took it, examined the keypad, punched a button. He held the instrument close to the microphone as an electronic chime sounded.

"On this trip, we'll be carrying a couple of these satellite phones,"

Donnelly said, holding the thing aloft. "They're not cheap—about four thousand dollars apiece—but they'll keep us in touch, wherever we go. Anything should happen—and it hasn't, yet—we can, at a moment's notice, call in a 'copter or whatever else might be necessary."

"Like a side of beef," Corrigan murmured. "Or more Pouilly-Fuissé."

Dara frowned to silence him, and Corrigan gave her a good-natured shrug.

Donnelly handed back the phone to his son and turned once again to the group. "Now, there'll be plenty of opportunity for the more adventurous among you to do some wild-game stalking—we shoot with cameras only, of course—and some rock climbing . . . " He paused to glance at Dawson, then continued: "And if you're really brave, maybe we'll let you put in the river a bit upstream from our normal spot, in case you want to get a taste of some wilder water." He paused again, waiting for some nervous laughter to die away.

"But I want to stress that you'll get your ration of thrilling experiences without having to be concerned for safety, beyond the reasonable precautions, of course. We've been at this for some years, now. I know the way in and the way out, and just in case I forget, we'll have our GPS along for good measure." He pointed back at Chipper again, who held up another electronic device a little smaller than a laptop computer. "If global positioning devices are good enough for Hertz and Avis," Donnelly said, "then they're good enough for us as well. Any other questions?" Donnelly called as the chuckles faded.

Corrigan longed to ask the man how he really felt about leading a bunch of tenderfeet through a fortnight of "wilderness experience," especially when the party had been assembled for the purpose of furthering a political campaign, but he knew he wouldn't. If he got the chance, maybe he'd ask Donnelly some version of the question over after-dinner drinks around the campfire.

For one thing, and despite all the Disneyesque overtones of the enterprise, Corrigan was beginning to look forward to seeing what was out there. For another, he suspected he knew the reasoning that lay at the heart of Donnelly's motivation. Avuncular Marlboro Man or no, Ben Donnelly surely loved the look of a healthy bank statement. For what he'd make from the trip, Corrigan thought, he'd probably be willing to escort Leona Helmsley through the territories.

"Well, if you all are through with me," Donnelly said, "then I'm through with you. I'll see you all out on the seaplane pier at eight A.M. sharp."

He left to a round of applause, and paused to accept a hearty handshake from Dawson. Waiters were hurrying toward the tables with dessert and coffee, but Dawson's entourage was up and filtering toward the door.

Corrigan turned to Dara, who was shaking her head at the offer of cheesecake.

"How about that drink?" he said.

She hesitated, then gave him a look. "I'm feeling a little worn out all of a sudden. Would you mind if I ducked out on you?"

He stared back at her. "Of course I would," he said. "But could I have a rain check?"

She nodded. "I'll buy you a drink in the mountains," she said. And then she gathered her things and was gone.

CHAPTER 13

LOST LAKE, IDAHO

The vast hangar was silent, the shapes of the planes dim silhouettes in the shadows. There was a vague nimbus of light that radiated from the cockpit of one of the craft, however, enough to draw the attention of the security man, who had been about to end his cursory inspection of the company offices, a small area in one corner of the building with its own entrance, a low, noninsulated roof of particleboard partitioned from the hangar itself by a wall that was framed primarily in glass.

The dog that was with him must have sensed something as well, possibly a nervous quality about the tug on its short chain lead, some tightening in the posture of its master, for it gave a low growl as the watchman doused his light and moved toward the door in the partitioned wall. "Quiet, Oscar," the man said, and the dog obeyed, even though it was trembling with anticipation as the two of them moved quietly out into the nearly dark hangar.

The smell of oil, grease, gasoline, and the indefinable musk of a cavernous structure that had housed machinery for many years rose to the man's nostrils. There was also something else in the air, something far less tangible though no less noticeable to the watchman, whose name was McCullough. Pressed to describe it, he would have called it trouble.

McCullough had been a night watchman, as he referred to himself, for only four months. Before that he had worked for almost a year at the Wal-Mart in Rock Springs, as a stocker and sales associate, until the company had dropped all but three—one per eight-hour shift—of its full-time employees in a cost-cutting move. Prior to that, he had worked for twenty-four years as a roustabout in the oil and gas fields in various forlorn spots around the West, a career that had ended when a load of drill casing burst its restraints and tumbled off a flatbed, shattering his left leg. The accident had left him with a limp, lingering arthritis in his knee and ankle, and an edge that hadn't helped him much in selling power tools and lawn mowers to penny-pinching idiots, but it was nothing his monthly disability check and a half-pint of Green Jack over the course of a lonely evening's tour of his present duties couldn't assuage.

The only fly in the ointment, so to speak, was the dog. McCullough had never liked dogs, considered them freeloaders on the great human enterprise at best, and the fact that this one actually had a job annoyed him all the more. He had learned, in fact, that the company that trained and provided the animals was paid a monthly sum for each that was greater even than his own salary. To be out-earned by a dog was a fact that he had labored mightily to accept.

"Hold on, you stupid shit," McCullough said in a fierce whisper, one hand tight on the animal's lead. He eased the door shut behind him and fished in his windbreaker pocket for the bottle. He spun the cap away with his thumb, palmed it, tipped the bottle for a taste, and had it down and capped again all in the space of time it might have taken John Elway to fire a short dump over the middle.

"All right," he hissed, nudging the dog with his knee. "Let's go see."

He could hear the animal's nails digging on the concrete floor, and, he supposed, so could anyone else who might happen to be in the building. Most likely, all this was for nothing. Most likely, the glow that lent a soft illumination to the cockpit up ahead was that of a panel light or a hand torch left on mistakenly by a crew member, but there was always the possibility of something else, some unfathomable skullduggery involved, and for McCullough, whose boredom had grown to gargantuan proportions over the past four months, the possibility of actually capturing someone up to no good filled him with an anticipatory rush that was very nearly sexual.

As it had, by all appearances, filled the straining animal as well. The thing was breathing in harsh pants, now, its nails tearing frantically at the floor. Though it pained him to think so, McCullough could not deny the notion that had flashed across the readout of his consciousness: *Good minds think alike.*

McCullough patted his chest, where he kept his pistol strapped, just to be sure. Intermountain Security supplied him with a nightstick, a leather sap, and a holstered can of Mace, but he had a registered permit to carry his own .38, and none of his supervisors had ever discouraged the practice. The West was still the West, after all.

As he came around the tail of the craft and noted the shadow of the gangway that extended down toward the hangar floor in the gesture of a languid hand, McCullough paused. He considered the possibility of another taste, briefly, then dismissed it. He reached to his shoulder holster, lifted out his pistol. He bent to the insanely straining dog and gave its skull a sharp rap with the butt of the weapon, careful to keep the barrel pointed away from his own skull just in case. The dog, to its credit, did not yelp; its struggles at the lead fell off considerably.

There was the problem of climbing the gangway to consider, but McCullough did not overthink the matter. He moved stealthily to the dangling steps, stepped around the dog, thumping it in the chest with his heel to make his intentions clear. The dog waited patiently for him to pass, and when it was time, moved nimbly up the metal steps behind McCullough about as quietly as was possible for a dog to do.

McCullough needed to climb less than halfway up to get a clear view inside the cockpit, and what he saw convinced him that all his suspicions had been dead-on from the beginning. A panel dangled loose from the copilot's console, wires splayed out like a network of arteries and veins. Some sort of trouble light had been rigged up there, hooked to a line that descended from the pilot's stick. Laid out on the floorboards was a set of what looked like dental tools in a soft leather case.

McCullough wasn't sure what was going on, but he knew he was not staring at the signs of scheduled maintenance. Sometimes work went on in the hangar after hours, but doors were open, overhead lights switched on, radios were played. McCullough realized that his hands had grown slick with sweat and that he was feeling a little light-headed. He drew his head back out of the cabin and stood unsteadily on the lower step of the gangway. He reholstered his pistol, then wiped his palms on his pants, transferring the dog's lead back and forth as he did so.

Whether the dog had heard something or had just taken advantage of the slackening in its lead as he passed it back and forth, McCullough couldn't say. In an instant, however, the lead had jerked from his hand and the animal was gone—no barks, no growls, just the frantic clatter of nails on concrete, receding into the darkness.

McCullough cursed, steadying himself on the wobbling gangway. The overpaid bastard was eager, he'd have to give it that much. And if the person who'd been mucking around, trying to steal valuable airplane instruments, was still in the building, McCullough felt sorry for him. The dog's powerful jaws had already been snapping viciously as it tore away.

He was down off the gangway, now, had his hand back on his pistol, when he heard the sounds: a muffled growl followed almost immediately by a great crashing of oil drums, part of the stack near the south hangar door, he calculated. McCullough was moving quickly in that direction, but had to duck as the shadow of a wing swooped up toward him out of the darkness.

Drums were still banging and rolling as he came up on the other side of the wing he'd nearly brained himself on. In a sliver of moonlight drifting in from the little see-through window in the delivery gate, he could make out the shapes of several of the big drums tumbled over, some of them still rocking back and forth. There was something else on the floor there, too, a broad dark puddle—oil, his mind insisted, had to be oil.

But there was something moving there in the middle of the puddle, something skittering and splashing and flopping like a beached fish. *What in God's name is a fish doing in an airplane hangar?* was the question that a part of McCullough's brain was demanding, but he chose to ignore it.

He squinted, cursing the dim light, then knelt down, cautious. Maybe it was a possum or a raccoon that had been nesting among those barrels, gotten squashed in all the ruckus. McCullough had his flashlight clipped to his belt, but something, some atavistic sense of self-preservation, was keeping him from snapping it on and making a sitting duck of himself in the darkness. Not until he knew a few more things.

Meantime, whatever it was flopping around there was about done for, he realized, its movements subdued, less frequent, now. He reached out gingerly with his pistol, nudged it. One last shuddering spasm, then nothing.

McCullough glanced over his shoulder. All quiet. Was the thing that had just died before him what had gotten the dog all worked up—some poor feral creature just looking for a quiet place to sleep?

And where *was* the fucking dog, anyway? McCullough turned back and used the barrel of his pistol to rake the inert form toward him, out of the dark puddle and into the slice of moonlight that painted the concrete floor.

What he saw made his heart lurch and caused his finger to tighten reflexively on the trigger of his pistol. The explosion blew hot fragments of concrete up against his cheeks, was magnified a dozen times over inside the cavernous hangar. McCullough was on his feet in an instant, staggering backward, slapping at his stinging cheeks. He was gasping for breath and trying to squeeze out little cries of terror at the same time.

Dog's head, he heard his mind saying as he danced backward from the awful thing he'd dragged into the light. *Dog's head. Dog's head. Dog's head.*

That flopping creature down there, that beached fish. *Sure, some poor possum, dumbass.* His legs were leaden, his throat the size of a pinhole. He had a pistol in his hand, but it might as well have been a rock or a snowball. He realized that his ears were still ringing, clogged, in fact, with a noise that went beyond a roar into some other realm. At first he assumed it was the echoing of the shot he'd fired, but in the next moment he realized it was something else altogether—some sound that was new, though still familiar.

He turned, staring dumbly into the dark reaches of the hangar. *Airplane,* he thought. *The roar of an airplane engine.*

He shook his head, trying to get himself under control. The sound was deafening, disorienting.

"Here!"

A voice. Very definitely a human voice, shouting over the roaring of the engines. McCullough felt his bowels going watery and at the same time remembered the pistol. He was holding it up, pointing it toward the ceiling like a starter about to kick off a race.

"Over here!" The voice, this time from a different angle. He spun about, dizzy, now, waving his pistol aimlessly before him. He felt a trickle of wetness at his cheek. His head was throbbing. A drum was rolling toward him. He sidestepped, his feet slipping in wetness.

"Here!" The voice again. He saw a shadow coming toward him and threw his arms up too late to stop it.

Something heavy struck him in the chest. His arms curled about it in reflex. Heavy and warm and wet, this burden he now clutched to his chest. The odor of wet fur. Of blood. Of sweetness and foulness and death.

McCullough realized he had lost his pistol. He was whimpering, choking on his own breath, beyond reason, beyond any hope of combat. He knew only that something, someone, was coming for him and that he longed to be anywhere else but there.

He turned and began to run, one step, a second, a third . . .

He realized he was still clutching the carcass of the dog to his chest, and flung it away with a cry of disgust. He was still moving, still praying the darkness might save him, when he remembered that the great roaring was in fact the sound of airplane engines and that the sudden and terrible wind whirling at his face might signal a great downturn in his prospects.

Had he thought these things a moment earlier, he might have stopped himself. For that matter, had he stayed himself from panic, he might not have run in the first place. He might have held his ground and used his pistol properly, and he might have come out of all this a hero.

But as it was, he was in full panic mode, in full flight, in midstep, and there was time to do nothing but fling up his arm as he toppled into the roaring, invisible cyclone just ahead.

"There must have been easier ways," she said.

"Never underestimate what a rent-a-cop might do," he told her.

"If you think I'm cleaning up that mess, you're crazy," she said.

"No one asked you to," he said.

"I just wanted to make sure," she said. "I've got plenty of work left of my own, you know."

"You do your thing, I'll do mine."

She shook her head, moved toward the still-swaying steps that climbed to the cockpit. "Just don't get any ideas," she said. "I'm going to be a while."

"Take as long as you need," he said, surveying the scene about him. At least they didn't have to worry about using the lights any longer. "I might just be a while myself."

CHAPTER

14

"It's a Grumman Mallard," Chipper was saying, pointing at the sizable seaplane that floated beside the pier nearby. "You ever been in one?"

Quite a speech for Chipper, Corrigan thought as he shook his head. He hadn't been looking at the plane, in fact. He'd been staring at the saw-toothed backdrop of the Tetons that loomed beyond the lake in the distance, as dramatic a sight as he'd ever seen.

He'd almost forgotten how chilly it was, he thought, unwrapping his parka-clad arms from in front of his chest. The sun was rising at his back, lighting the tips of the mountains in brilliant gold, leaving their lower reaches in blue-black shadow, and it already seemed ten degrees warmer. He gave an experimental puff of breath from his cheeks, noticed that no vapor took shape, and tried to force himself to pay attention to the outfitter's son standing beside him.

The mountains' reflections seemed to stretch across the intervening water toward him, though a breeze had kicked up and a light chop had sent the inverted images dancing into an impressionist's dream. The waves sloshed against the hull of the plane with a hollow sound, and

Corrigan made himself turn to face Chipper, this earnest young man who'd taken a break from his supervision of the loading of the gear and only wanted to talk.

"Looks like a boat with wings," Corrigan said. Unlike smaller seaplanes Corrigan had seen in pictures, this craft's hull rested squarely on the water. The pontoon structures, which dangled from the tips of the wings, seemed barely to touch the water.

Chipper nodded. "That's about what it is," he said. "Those floats at the end of the wings are really auxiliary fuel tanks. We can put another fifty gallons in each one."

"I guess that's important," Corrigan said.

"This little puppy burns a hundred gallons an hour, loaded the way she is," Chipper said. "The regular tanks'll hold four hundred. She goes about a hundred and fifty knots, assuming there's no headwind. So that's plenty of fuel to get us where we're going and get the pilot back home." Chipper gave him an affable glance. "Still, you like to have yourself a margin for error, flying around this country."

Corrigan wasn't sure he wanted to ask about what might constitute "error," and he had the uncomfortable feeling that Chipper was about to tell him. "You had it long?"

"Naw, we just lease it on a need-be basis," he said. "There's an outfit up in Idaho we get 'em from."

"That where they're made, Idaho?" Corrigan was starting to get the hang of this patter. Just drift along from one inconsequential thing to another, maybe you learn something useful, maybe you don't. A lot like passing the time of day with another cop, he thought.

He glanced back toward shore where the big Chevy Blazer sat, Dara in there, talking to Dawson.

"They don't make a Mallard anywhere, not anymore," Chipper was saying. "This one was 1948, I think."

Corrigan looked at him, his attention finally caught. "It's fifty years old?" he said, hearing the surprise in his own voice.

Chipper shrugged. "I wouldn't be too concerned. There's a whole airline still uses them down in Florida," he said. "Chalk's. Takes people from Miami all around the Caribbean. They tell me Jimmy Buffett has one, too."

"It doesn't look fifty years old," Corrigan said. The part about Jimmy Buffett failed to reassure him. Unless he was mistaken, every rock-and-roll star of the fifties and sixties seemed to have died in a small-plane crash. Buffett could simply be thumbing his nose at Fate.

"They're well taken care of," Chipper said, a smile forming at the corners of his mouth. "Totally refurbished, the engines replaced altogether in the seventies, when a guy named Frakes came up with the idea of adding turbo props. The Coast Guard uses 'em for air-sea rescue in weather they'd never take a helicopter out in."

"We don't have to talk about rescue, do we?"

"Not if you don't want to," Chipper said.

After a moment, he turned his gaze toward the Blazer. "She's a pretty girl, isn't she?"

Corrigan looked to see if Chipper might be goading him, but there was nothing like guile on his round face. Give it a few years, let the wind and the rain and the sun go to work on that visage, maybe something like his old man's "Been there, done that, seen it all" expression would take shape. Right now, he was just a guy expressing what every other guy in his right mind would express, or so Corrigan thought.

"She *is* a piece of work," Corrigan said. And they both nodded at that, just as one of the doors of the Blazer opened and a peal of Fielding Dawson's laughter rolled out their way.

Seventeen seats, seventeen passengers, Corrigan noted as the plane taxied out toward takeoff. He was sitting in one of the single places near the rear, where the cabin narrowed, and he'd had plenty of time to count. Up front were Dawson and his wife, Elizabeth, the Ashmeads, and Dawson's assistant, Ariel Sorenson—an energetic young woman with plum-colored lipstick and matching dark nails who looked like she survived on a diet of wheat germ and positive thoughts. There was also the muscle-bound type who'd been with Soldinger at the airport, the last remnant of real "security," Corrigan supposed. Soldinger, it was explained, had gone off to make arrangements for the governor's press conference at the other end of the line.

Behind Dawson's entourage, Donnelly and Chipper sat together, intently trading comments over a topographical map. Close by were two other wiry, leather-skinned types who looked like they'd been flown in from wrangler central.

From Chipper, he'd learned that there were five members of the film team: a young female director who'd done a number of documentaries for the Adventure Channel, two cameramen, a sound man, and a grip. That group had clustered together as well, leaving Corrigan and Dara the last seats: Dara sat across the narrow aisle in another single place, intent on her notes.

Corrigan turned his own attention out the window. The wind seemed to have picked up, and the plane wallowed in the chop, its engines groaning louder. Though he couldn't make out the shoreline from his angle, he sensed that they had been taxiing or trolling or whatever a seaplane did for way long enough to reach their takeoff point.

Earlier, Chipper had broken off his discourse on the Mallard's features long enough for Dara to make her way past them and on toward the plane, but the moment she was out of sight, he'd relapsed. Corrigan had learned that the plane needed a good 5,000 feet of unobstructed waterway in order to take off or land. ("Don't worry, we got seven thousand feet here, and a good six thousand up in the mountains.") That much had sounded vaguely reassuring, until Chipper began to explain how payload and altitude could affect these limits.

"We'll put down at just about nine thousand feet," he'd said, shaking his head. "Air's awful thin up that high, so you *need* some extra room."

Corrigan tried to put such thoughts aside, feeling the pulsation of the engines growing. He felt a momentary surge of anxiety, then came the moment of release as the plane started forward, lumbering through the water at first as if it were trying to plow through glue. In moments, the pace had quickened, doubling and redoubling until they were skimming the wave tops. Finally they were lifting free of the water altogether and were airborne. In the next moment, the plane had banked steeply, laying out the breathtaking sight of the Tetons before him.

"Awesome," Corrigan heard himself saying. It was not a word he was inclined to use, but what else could he say?

"Leave it to a Frenchman to name them breasts." Dara's voice came to him.

He turned to see her leaning across the aisle, sharing his view. He might have said something, but he wasn't quite sure what she was talking about.

"*Grand Tetons,*" she said, by way of explanation. "As in *big breasts.*"

"Oh," Corrigan said.

"Don't tell me," she said, "you hadn't thought about what the name meant."

"I guess I never thought about it," he told her. He wasn't sure if his face was coloring or if it was just the sudden shift in altitude. All he could think about suddenly were *her* breasts. It took a monumental force of his will not to stare.

"This the kind of place you grew up in?" he asked after a moment.

She looked up at him, seemed to decide something. She put her notebook aside, glanced out the window. "Not exactly. Salt Lake's an actual city, you know."

"But you're not a Mormon."

"Is this an interrogation?"

"Just making conversation," he said.

She nodded, leaned back in her seat. "My father taught journalism at the university in Salt Lake City," she said. "He grew up Methodist in Odessa, Texas, but he believed in the Gospel according to Damon Runyon."

She tucked a lock of her hair behind her ear, and he thought she looked tired, suddenly. He didn't like thinking of her that way. He preferred bright and cheery. "How'd you get to New York?" he asked.

"You really want to know?"

He nodded. *That and a few thousand other things,* he thought.

She glanced across the narrow aisle at him. "After I graduated, I moved to Southern California with a couple of girls from school, to get away from home. I was knocking around, trying to get on with the *Times,* had picked up some work as a stringer for *USA,* when the O.J. story broke. As it turned out, I was going to the same health club where one of his girlfriends was a member. I knew this girl on a first-name basis, we were doing the StairMasters together one day, and out of nowhere she burst into tears, started telling me all this stuff about what she really believed about what he'd done."

A rueful smile crossed her face. "Some reporter I am. After a couple of minutes, I'm going, like, 'Oh, she's *that* Paula!'"

Corrigan considered it for a moment and glanced ahead toward Dawson and the others. "You're telling me you're the one who spilled this girl's mess in *USA Magazine,* therefore I can trust you not to get me in trouble?"

She shook her head. "Other people got into that part of her story. The piece I did was all about the real person behind all the headlines. I didn't write one thing she was upset with." She fixed him with her stare. "Anyway, you asked me a question, I'm answering you truthfully. I wrote that story, the L.A. bureau chief offered me a full-time job with the magazine. When he got the New York bureau last year, I asked to come along. So here I am." She flashed him her ingenuous smile, gesturing at the rugged terrain below. "Back in the wilderness."

Corrigan nodded. "So, what was it you wanted to discuss with me, anyway? I have to warn you, though, it's not like Fielding Dawson told me where he hid his bloody gloves."

"It doesn't have anything to do with Dawson," she said.

"I already told you I can't talk about what happened down there that day."

"I know," she said, turning to him. There was a mournful expression on her face, he thought.

"Then what?"

"I'm sure no one else knows this . . ." she began.

"I'll say this much," he told her impatiently. "You know how to string a story out."

She didn't smile. "Remember I told you I did that piece on the subways?"

"Maybe I remember something." He shrugged.

"Well," she said, "one of the things that never got in the story was this sidebar I wanted to add about some of the homeless people still living down there."

"There's a lot of them," he said. "There used to be a lot more?"

She nodded. "And some of them are pretty interesting," she said. "They've had some fairly amazing experiences."

"So I have observed," he said.

"I mean, *before* they ended up down there," she said.

"I know there is a point to all this," Corrigan said.

She'd been biting her lip. Finally she glanced to be sure no one seemed to be listening, then leaned closer to him. "The point is, I think I know who the man was that you . . ." She broke off, then continued, "The man who died."

He was shaking his head. "How could you know? He wasn't carrying any I.D. The M.E. couldn't even find a set of teeth. They'll never find out who that guy was."

"I can't be sure," she persisted. "But judging from his height, the way he moved and all . . ."

"How in the hell would you know what he looked like—" He broke off suddenly, staring at her as it sunk in. "You talked to Montcrief, didn't you. You pumped Rollie about all this . . ."

"Richard," she said, shaking her head, "I was just doing my job. I'd been assigned to the governor's campaign—"

"Sonofabitch," he said. "What're you trying to do, break the big story of the killer cave cop?"

She stared at him, her eyes wide. "I don't know what you're talking about. You're not in any trouble that I'm aware of."

"Then what the hell *are* we talking about?"

She sighed. "I wasn't even going to bring it up, okay? But the more I thought about it, the more it bothered me."

He forced himself to calm down, tried to focus on the steady grinding noise of the plane's engines. "Just tell me. Who is this guy you think you know?" He was ready for anything at this point. The guy had once played for the Knicks. Had invented the computer chip. He was the second fucking gunman behind the grassy knoll.

"He was nobody special," she said quietly. "Or he was, depending on how you view it. He'd been a teacher. A philosophy professor, for a time. He had some pretty unusual ideas. I suppose that's why he ended up losing his job. He'd been married, had a son and a daughter—he had no idea what had happened to them, of course. He'd been hospitalized. There was drinking, a drug problem . . ." She broke off, biting her lip again.

"Look, Richard, I don't even know why I'm telling you all this. I—"

He raised his hand to stop her. "I think you know exactly why you're telling me. You think you've got a pretty good story here, but telling it would run against the grain of your big assignment with the governor up there, and you don't know whether it's worth the trouble until you see what's doing with the big hero cop."

She was shaking her head, ready to interrupt, but he wasn't about to give her the chance. "Well, let me make it easy for you," he said. "Let me be the first to deliver the scoop."

"Richard—"

"All this about me saving the governor's life is bullshit," he said.

She stared at him, shaking her head uncertainly.

"Shots fired, hand-to-hand combat," he said, gesturing toward the front of the plane. "It never happened. The poor bastard never even had a gun."

"But your partner said he did—"

"It might have looked like it when he came out of the bushes," Corrigan said. "What he was holding was a piece of plastic. This homeless philosopher you interviewed, he have a problem with asthma?"

"I saw a copy of the police report," she insisted, holding her voice low. "A thirty-two-caliber pistol—"

"Somebody threw it down," Corrigan said.

She stared back at him in shock.

"It wasn't me," he added. "I was chasing the guy down onto the platform; he tripped and fell before I could catch him. End of story." He paused. "The rest of it just sort of grew."

"Like Topsy," she said, still shaking her head.

"Like a lot of things," he said, gesturing toward the front of the plane. "So, here I am, Fielding Dawson's chief show pony, just the way you called it. How's that for a story?"

There was a long pause.

"Pretty sad," she said finally.

"I couldn't agree more," he said.

"You remember I said I was sorry your father had died?" she said after a moment.

"Yeah. What's that have to do with it?"

"Because I think you'd like to have him here to talk to right now."

"We didn't talk about much when he was alive."

"Still," she said. "Still."

He felt a deep ache growing somewhere under his lungs. "You talk to your old man about what stories to write?"

She shook her head. "He's dead, too. Heart attack. Right in front of his class one day."

He paused. "Your mom?"

She shook her head. "She didn't last too long after he died."

He forced himself to take a breath. A doozy of a deep breath, this time. "So, what would your old man think about what I just gave you?"

She thought about it. "He'd probably tell me to trust my own instincts."

"What do *they* tell you?"

She held his gaze. "That you're a good guy," she said, glancing out the window. "And that we're about to land."

He turned as a jolt of rough air caused him to clutch reflexively at the armrests of his seat. He glanced out, saw that they were pushing into a bank of clouds.

". . . little rough weather as we make our approach." The voice of the pilot crackled over the intercom. "Just be sure to stay buckled tight. . . ."

If he'd intended to say something else, Corrigan couldn't be sure, for his attention had been drawn away by a sudden, sickening drop in their altitude, followed by an equally sharp surge upward. He kept his grip on the armrests but felt his seatbelt pull tightly against his midsection, felt his head fly back, then dip, as if he were on some carnival ride. He glanced up at the ceiling of the plane, listening as the engines picked up a notch in volume. If he hadn't been buckled in, he thought, he would have surely bounced off those unyielding-looking panels.

Then, just as quickly, they had broken out of the clouds. As if by magic, the ride steadied and sunshine poured through the windows. Dazed by the sudden contrast, Corrigan glanced out and saw another range of snowcapped peaks in the distance.

". . . about the joyride." The still-crackling voice of the pilot came again. "But we'll be down in a minute. . . ." More crashing and hissing, then, and the roar of the engines kicked up yet another notch.

The plane was dropping through a pass between peaks, now, a green canopy spread about below, with a view of sheer granite cliffs out either window. There was snow still packed in the recesses of the mountains and, here and there, waterfalls tumbling toward the forest below.

He strained to see the bottom of the canyon beneath them, and did manage to make out one brief flash of white water far below. He wondered if that was the route they'd take on the last leg of their journey, or if it might be just one of a multitude of white-water rivers in this exotic land. He saw a dark shape rushing across the sun-washed shoulder of mountain nearby, and realized that it was the shadow of their plane hurtling along.

Abruptly they were soaring over a rock-strewn ridge, and their hurrying shadow had vanished. Ahead, Corrigan caught a glimpse of forest, then a crescent of blue mirroring an array of snow peaks. It was so perfect—as pristine as one of those perfect-looking shots from a drugstore calendar—that he found it impossible to accept at first.

But then the plane banked for its final descent, allowing him another look at the lake and the mountains and the encircling canopy of pines, and he knew that it was true, that they had arrived. Say what you might about Fielding Dawson and the reasons for this trip, Richard Corrigan believed he was staring out now at paradise.

The plane turned again, its flaps dropping, its engines groaning a deeper note as the drag increased. In moments, it seemed, they had dropped below the rocky line of the ridge and were whisking over the tops of the pines, the glassy surface of the lake looming up ahead.

He knew it was only an illusion created by his faulty sense of perspective as he glanced at the encroaching pines and looming peaks, but the plane actually seemed to be picking up speed as they arrowed toward the water. Numbers born of Chipper's monologue on altitude and landing clearances flashed through his mind with no regard for logic: Did they need 26,000 feet to land, or was that the height of some Himalayan peak? Was the lake below 9,000 feet deep, or 150 knots wide? Did anyone care?

He felt a moment of dizzying lunacy—*If this is how it ends, then what a way to go*—and then the plane kissed the water. They bounced up briefly like a huge stone skimming the surface, then came down again, this time hugging the water for good. A spontaneous cheer arose in the cabin, and Corrigan realized that he had lent his voice to the cry.

"**Is this real?**" Corrigan said to Dara. They were still on the pier that reached out into the lake, watching as the seaplane taxied away for its takeoff. The breeze off the lake was cool, the thin air exhilarating, the early sun hot on his forehead.

She glanced around, smiling. "About as real as it gets," she said, her voice softening.

"What are those?" he asked, pointing at a pair of sizable rodentlike creatures scuttling along the rocky shore.

She followed his gesture. "Marmots," she said.

"A better-looking grade of rat?"

She gave him a look. "More like a squirrel," she said.

"We could introduce them into the subways," he said. "Upgrade the neighborhood."

She shook her head, smiling.

"I guess you've seen a lot of places like this, growing up out West," he continued.

She gave him an appraising stare. "Nothing any prettier than this," she said.

He nodded. "You forget, where I come from, Central Park is a vast, unspoiled wilderness."

"Central Park is pretty, too."

He glanced toward shore, where Donnelly and his crew were busying themselves arranging gear. One of the wranglers—Vaughn was his name—had already started a fire and had put up a pot of coffee. Corrigan, who sometimes had coffee and sometimes not, could smell the aroma all the way to the end of the dock.

The other wrangler—Pete, was it?—was fitting together some fly rods for the morning amusement of Dawson and his friends, Corrigan assumed. The plan, as Donnelly had outlined it, was to have lunch where they were, then spend the afternoon in a leisurely trek around to the far side of the lake, where the waterfall tumbled down. They'd camp there for the evening, then strike out over the ridge and on into the wilderness first thing in the morning.

He turned, found Dara holding a camera toward him. "I'm supposed to leave the photography to the other team—Dawson will clear everything through them—but I don't suppose anyone would care about a couple of snapshots," she said. "If you don't mind, that is."

He gave her a look. "I'm not much good at it," he said. And he never had been, he thought, suspecting it had something to do with his eye.

"I trust you," she said, her gaze holding his.

He took the camera, waved at the crystal water. "What kind of fish are in here, anyway?"

"Trout," she said, with the hint of a smile. "Remember trout?"

"Roger on the trout," he said. He could still see her wielding her dinner knife, deftly lifting that latticework of bones away.

Corrigan noticed that Dawson had taken up one of the fly rods and was waving it in erratic loops. Maybe he should try to place Dara in the foreground, try his best to catch the governor in some preposterous great-hunter pose in the background, he was thinking, when he heard the revving of the seaplane at the far end of the lake, and hesitated.

"Maybe I ought to take a picture of the plane taking off," he said to Dara. "Departure of our last link to civilization and all that?"

She shrugged. "Suit yourself."

"Move right over here," he said, motioning her toward the edge of the pier.

He steadied himself against one of the pilings, tried to focus on her and get the revving plane there in the background. He heard the pitch of the engines climb as he maneuvered the focus, saw a tiny storm of white-caps kick up in the wash of the propellers.

He remembered back a few hours before, when he'd sat white-knuckled inside the same craft, waiting for that precise moment of release, when the urge to be aloft overcame the instinct to clutch hold, no matter what . . . and it occurred to him, staring at Dara through the lens, that he wished there was a way to capture such a feeling on film.

It was a luxuriant experience, having this excuse just to stare at her, the first chance he'd really dared to since he'd spotted her unaware, back at that press conference. He held up his hand to signal her, snapped one shot as the plane's engines grew in volume, another as they finally released. He caught a glimpse of the plane as it hurtled away, a rogue wave slapping the tail as if to finish a game of got-you-last.

He got another good shot of her with the snowy peaks in the background, shifted slightly, and took another.

"I think that's probably enough, Richard," she said.

"Just a couple more," he said, eye still pressed to the viewfinder.

Her face, the feeling of flight, the icy water, and the plane gleaming in the sun, a graceful white arrow against the dark backdrop of the cliff, where water drifted like shaken lace.

"Richard." He heard Dara's voice as he snapped, and snapped again, turning to catch the rest of the view.

"Richard, I think something's wrong."

He heard the concern, finally noted it in her face, wondered what she might be talking about, what could be wrong.

Be right with you, he was thinking. *Just one second more.*

Yes, yes, yes, he thought with each snap of the shutter. He had it, he was certain, now. He dropped the camera at last and turned to see what, in Dara's world, the trouble was, at the instant it became abundantly clear.

The explosion, magnified several times over by the surrounding rock walls, ripped across the surface of the lake like the clap of doom itself. An enormous fireball shot up the face of the cliff, obliterating the water-fall for a brief moment. In the aftermath, bits of wreckage rained down upon the lake in an awful hailstorm.

And then, suddenly, all was calm again. For a few moments, time was stilled. No sound of laboring engines, no screams of onlookers. The echoes of the explosion had died away. No scar upon the wall of rock where the water tumbled, nothing left on the calm surface of the lake.

No evidence whatsoever of what had just taken place, not to Corri-gan's eyes. He stood frozen, the camera dangling, gaping out over the empty water, feeling Dara's hands clutching at his arm, trying to com-prehend.

It can't be, something in him insisted. *Impossible. Absolutely, cate-gorically impossible.*

From somewhere in the tall pines behind him came one note, the raucous call of a crow. And then, from all about him, the disbelieving cries began.

The tall man listened as the echoes of the explosion rolled away, then glanced down at the tiny transmitter he still held in his hand. With its various arrowed buttons and switches, it might have been mistaken for a sophisticated video-game controller. Except that this was one capable of guiding much more than computerized images, he thought. Receiver there, transmitter here—you could take over the electronic guidance of just about any craft. So clever, these Japanese.

He put the device back into a pocket, and turned to make his way back down the trail beneath the trees toward the campsite, careful of his footing in the sandy soil. Every pebble, every shard of wood was a tiny, old-fashioned disaster-in-waiting, and electronics was no shield. Twist an ankle, break a bone out here, it could mean your life. Particularly if you were alone.

He was not alone, of course, but he would behave as if he were. It was the best way. For him, the only way.

The woman glanced up when she heard his approach, her face spangled with sunlight and shadow cast by the pines. She had her long hair tied back in a knot, a kerchief around her neck. No makeup, a loose-fitting T-shirt, blousy camper's pants. See her in the city, you might take her for a wheat-germ lady, a tree-hugger, a nature nerd. And God help you if you did.

She'd been on her knees, shoveling the last of the soil back atop the hole he'd helped her dig. She stood, now, tossing the camp shovel aside, wiping a sheen of sweat from her brow.

"That sound I heard a bit ago," she asked. She gestured toward the top of the ridge where he'd been. "Was it what I think it was?"

He nodded, still staring at the partner Fate had brought him.

"I expect they're about to try their fancy satellite phone devices," she added.

"I expect they are," he said.

"So, let the games begin," she said with a last glance at the silent mound beside her.

And with that, they started off.

CHAPTER 15

"Where's that goddamned phone?" Ben Donnelly shouted toward his son over the turmoil at lakeside.

Chipper had plowed into the stack of gear piled near the pier head. He finished rummaging through one rucksack, tossed it aside, turned his attention to the next. "It was in there. I *know* it was."

He glanced up at Corrigan, who'd just hurried in from the pier.

"Take it easy," Corrigan said. "You'll find it."

Chipper gave him a doubtful look, but in the next instant his face brightened. He withdrew his hand from the canvas bag, held the phone up in triumph.

Donnelly strode forward and snatched the device from Chipper's hand. He pressed a button, started to punch in numbers, then abruptly stopped.

He tried again, then turned the phone over and flipped open a compartment on the back. "Where's the battery?" he said to Chipper.

Chipper shook his head. "I don't know. It was there yesterday when I packed it. It had to be."

Donnelly scowled. "Where's the other phone?" he barked at Chipper.

"Maybe you took it," Chipper said.

"I didn't take the goddamned thing . . ." Donnelly began, then cut himself off.

"Get my pack," he said to one of the wranglers.

The wrangler found Donnelly's pack amid the stack of gear, jerked it loose, hurried forward with it. Donnelly set the bag on the rocks at his feet, then bent down to paw through the contents.

After a moment he stopped, glancing up briefly at his son. He reached into the bag with his other hand, brushed aside some clothing, and pulled out a second phone, the twin to the first. He turned the phone over and checked the battery pack. He pressed a button, and the electronic chime Corrigan had heard at the briefing the night before sounded faintly in the thin mountain air.

A look approaching relief spread across Donnelly's face, and he turned to punch in a series of numbers on the keypad. He brought the phone to his ear, then, waiting for the connection to be made.

Corrigan stared about them at the array of silent faces. Sixteen people standing by the side of a lake in the middle of nowhere, watching a man make a telephone call, he thought. Somehow it seemed ludicrous.

Dara must have felt something similar. "Shouldn't we try to get over there?" she said, holding her voice down. She gestured at the spot where the plane had exploded. "See if someone might have made it?"

Corrigan turned to her, mindful of Donnelly's unfortunate example. "It'd take hours," he said, gesturing at the rugged shoreline that lay between them and the crash site. "I'm not sure there's much point in it."

"But we can't just stand here like ghouls," she said.

"Hold it down," Donnelly called. "I can't hear." He listened a moment, then banged the phone against his palm in frustration. He pressed another button, seemingly clearing the call, then punched in numbers once again.

"For God's sake," he said after a moment. He pulled the phone away from his ear again, glaring at Corrigan, who stood closest to him.

"What?" Corrigan asked, shaking his head.

"You listen," Donnelly said, thrusting the phone at him.

Corrigan reached out and brought the phone carefully to his ear. Unintelligible clamor, at first, but then it began to resolve itself into recognizable sound. Finally he pulled the instrument from his ear and stared back at Donnelly.

"Sounds like Japanese radio to me," Donnelly said, his voice disgusted.

Corrigan nodded. He'd heard the same excited chatter, then music swelling up, the sounds tinny but unmistakable: a group from somewhere far away, pumping out the strains of an old Beatles tune in Oriental harmony. And, unless he missed his guess, what they were calling for was "Help!"

CHAPTER

16

"The batteries to one phone disappear, the other one picks up only Japanese radio? Is that some kind of joke?" Dara said to him.

Corrigan shrugged. "If it is, it's a pretty grim one," he said. They stood in the shade of some pines a few yards up from the lakeshore while Donnelly, who'd tried the remaining phone several more times without success, conferred with Dawson.

Odd, Corrigan thought, rubbing his arms against the chill breeze. Out in the sun, it had seemed hot. A few minutes in the shade and he was practically shivering, but then again, he could see pockets of snow still lurking here and there, sheltered by rock outcroppings and pines. "Just like those new phones they okayed for the Transit Authority cops," he said, checking the sky. The sun was well up over the mountains to the east, but clouds had begun scudding in, and large patches of shadow were gliding over the surface of the lake. "They were going to revolutionize communications underground, according to the hype."

Dara nodded glumly. "How about that GPS device Donnelly showed us at dinner last night?" she asked.

Corrigan glanced at her. "We know where we *are,* Dara. That's all a thing like that is good for."

She shook her head, glancing across the lake toward the waterfall, as beautiful, as indifferent, as ever. "Those poor men."

He nodded, remembering all of Chipper's technical jargon about altitudes and takeoff and landing clearances, remembered his own death's grip on the armrests of his seat. "A few minutes the other way, it could have been all of us," he told her with a bleak look.

They stood quietly for a moment, staring out over the water, while the conference between Donnelly and Dawson continued down by the water. Donnelly was making an effort at keeping his voice down, but Corrigan could hear the strain in the man's voice. By the agitated way Donnelly moved, Corrigan guessed there was some disagreement between the pair, though what it might be was anyone's guess. Was Dawson blaming Donnelly for the accident, for the malfunctioning phones? Could a plane crash affect a candidate's poll numbers adversely?

"So, what happens now?" Dara asked over his shoulder.

"I'm not sure," Corrigan said. "When the plane doesn't show up back in Jackson, it'll raise some flags. They'll send a search plane out."

"So, that's it? We'll just wait here to get picked up?"

He gave her a blank look. "I suppose. I'm not exactly the one in charge."

She stared back at him, her expression despairing. "Hardly what anyone had in mind, is it?"

He shook his head, glancing out at the end of the pier where the film crew had huddled, each caught up in formulating his own battle plan, he supposed. Giles Ashmead stood together with his wife, Sonia, a few feet from Dawson and Donnelly, while Dawson's own private linebacker and his female assistant hovered nearby. Corrigan noted that the young woman's plum-colored nails and lips, which might have seemed stylish once, now only accentuated her pallor.

Chipper and the two wranglers were busy rearranging the gear, moving it away from the water's edge, closer to the encircling forest. Elizabeth Dawson had walked out to the end of the pier and stood with her arms wrapped about herself, as if she were fighting some deep chill, her back to them all.

Finally Corrigan turned back to Dara, trying to find some reassuring words, when Donnelly's voice cut through his intentions. "Heads up, folks," the outfitter called. "I need everyone's attention, please. On down here, if you would."

Everyone began to filter Donnelly's way. Even Elizabeth Dawson seemed eager enough to end her exile, had turned, and was making her way quickly back along the pier.

When they all had gathered sufficiently close, Donnelly raised his hands and began. "I know we've suffered a terrible tragedy, here, and I want to commend everyone on how well you've taken it, that's the first thing."

He glanced off toward the cliff where the plane had crashed, then turned back to them. "I've known Don Barton for most of my adult life, and I've put my life in his hands more times than I can count. He was as good as they come." He paused, shaking his head in sorrow. "I don't have the slightest idea what happened up there, but I know that Don would be the first one to say he'd rather it was him and not us."

"What are we going to do?" It was the director of the film crew. Her mascara seemed smudged, as if she might have been crying.

Donnelly nodded, anticipating the question. "Well, I presume you all realize we've got a foul-up with our communications." He sent a dark look toward Chipper, as if his son were responsible for the failure of all things modern.

"Now, maybe that'll clear itself up yet," Donnelly continued, his voice rising to carry above the growing sigh of the wind through the pines. "If it does, we'll call in immediately and report the crash."

"When the plane doesn't return to the airport on schedule," Corrigan offered, "won't they send out a search party?"

Donnelly cleared his throat, looking distinctly uncomfortable. "Ordinarily, that's exactly what would happen. We could just wait right here, send up a flare the minute we see a plane—"

"But that's not going to happen anytime soon." It was Fielding Dawson cutting in, clearly impatient with Donnelly's elliptical manner. The governor strode forward, gazing about the group. "The plane wasn't flying directly back to Jackson. It was on its way to a remote lake in southern Montana to rendezvous with a group of fishermen the day after tomorrow."

"The day after tomorrow?" Giles Ashmead said in disbelief. "Then it could be two days, maybe three, before anyone raises an alarm. . . ."

So, that explained Dawson's obvious irritation, Corrigan thought. He turned to Donnelly. "This lake in Montana, is it as isolated as the place we are now?"

Donnelly glanced around, made a helpless gesture. "Well, not *quite* as isolated as here, but Heggen Lake's still a couple days' hike in or out."

"And how about *that* group?" Corrigan persisted. "How many functioning satellite phones do they have?"

Donnelly shook his head. "Tell you the truth, it isn't one of my groups, Mr. . . . ?" He paused, looking uncertainly at Corrigan.

"Corrigan," he said. "Richard Corrigan."

"Right," Donnelly said. "You're the police officer."

Corrigan gave him a grudging nod.

"Well," Donnelly said, "the plane was leased from a company that hires out to a number of outfitters in these parts."

Corrigan nodded. It was as Chipper had suggested earlier, then. "So, even if this group of fishermen on Lake Whatever-It-Is realizes that something has happened to the plane that was supposed to pick them up, they might be in the same position we are. Nothing to do but wait and wonder."

"Up shit's creek without a paddle," one of the cameramen offered.

"Who knows *how* long we'll have to wait for help," Sonia Ashmead said, her attractive features pained.

Here, Donnelly broke in, perhaps sensing a stampede. "Well, the fact is, we don't exactly need *help*, Mrs. Ashmead." He glanced back at Dawson. "What's happened is unfortunate . . ."

Probably not the words the two pilots might have used, Corrigan thought, but he kept that to himself.

". . . but we're in pretty good shape, truth be told. We've got our gear, we've got our original game plan intact." Donnelly cleared his throat again, giving Dawson a sidelong glance. "What Mr. Dawson and I have determined is that we might just as well start making our own way back down toward civilization—"

"Wait a minute," Elizabeth Dawson said. "I thought it was going to take the better part of a week to get out of this"—she turned, waving her arm about their surroundings—"this hellhole!"

"Well, we can shave some time off that figure, Mrs. Dawson," Donnelly said, clearly uncomfortable. Corrigan suspected the outfitter had been privy to some of Elizabeth Dawson's thoughts on the beauties of the wilderness before this moment. "With any luck, we can be out of here in as little as three days. . . ."

"Three days?" she said, her voice rising even higher.

"Meantime," Donnelly said, holding up a hand to forestall whatever she intended to say, "we'll send Chipper and Pete over there on ahead. They can move twice as fast as all of us together can. It's even money they'll be able to get down, get the word out about what's happened, before that group up in Montana even realizes there's been a problem."

Fielding Dawson spoke up at this point. "I think we should all remind ourselves that, in fact, there is no problem where we personally are concerned. . . ."

"If the point is to get us all back to civilization as quickly and painlessly as possible, then maybe we ought to stay put until help arrives, whether that's two days, or three, or four." Corrigan turned to regard the film crew. "I know that pretty much does away with the point of the trip—"

"That's hardly the issue, Officer Corrigan," Dawson interrupted. "The truth is, we *can't* stay here."

"And why is that?" Corrigan asked.

Dawson glanced at Donnelly, inviting the outfitter to do the explaining.

"For one thing, we don't have enough supplies, and we're not really outfitted for serious hunting or fishing," Donnelly said, loud enough for everyone to hear. "We need to get down the mountainside to the first cache point, or there are going to be a bunch of hungry people among you."

Corrigan thought he heard Elizabeth Dawson mutter a curse. If he noticed, Donnelly ignored it. He ran his gaze over the group, then turned back to Corrigan and nodded upward. "For another thing, we've got the weather to think about."

Corrigan glanced up at the sky, where the clouds had thickened considerably. In the distance, over the peaks, it appeared that dark thunderheads were brewing. "That's just rain right now. But if a bad enough storm comes through at this altitude," Donnelly explained, "we could find ourselves up to our butts in snow, even in September. It behooves us to move a little lower down the mountainside."

Behooves? As Corrigan stared at the man, Dara broke in: "Don't you check the weather before you start off on these things?"

"Of course we do," Donnelly shot back. "But storms kick up. Things happen in the wilderness. That's why we want to get moving." He broke off to survey the group.

"Well, you've heard the plan. So, unless there are any other questions . . ."

He waited for a moment, but no one else spoke up. "The boys'll rustle up a quick lunch," Donnelly said, motioning toward the fire, where

Pete and Vaughn were already busy. "And then we'll be on our way." He stole one last glance toward the gathering skies. "I'd keep my poncho out where I could get to it, you all," he added, and then turned away, one hand on Fielding Dawson's shoulder.

Dawson gave Corrigan something of a speculative glance, then followed Donnelly away toward the fire, where Pete and Vaughn were adding seasonings and feathery-looking dried vegetables to a pot Corrigan supposed held soup. Corrigan, who realized his gut had tightened into a knot over the last few minutes, let out his breath in a rush. So maybe he'd annoyed Fielding Dawson, he thought, but at least he'd forced Donnelly into an admission that there were legitimate concerns about their situation.

"I'm not sure he liked your implication," Dara said.

Corrigan turned. "What implication?"

"Suggesting Dawson doesn't want to miss his photo opportunity," she said.

"That's not what I said."

"But I think you hit the nail on the head," she said, with the hint of a smile. "You let him off easy, in fact."

"I'm just a public servant," he said. "You're the reporter. Why don't you hold his feet to the fire?"

She glanced at the governor, then shrugged. "There's no rush," she said. "Let's see how things turn out."

Corrigan glanced at Dawson, who was now standing near the campfire, engaged in earnest conversation with Giles Ashmead and his wife. He noted that Elizabeth Dawson had not joined the group but had wandered off once again toward the lakeside, her arms wrapped about herself as if she were warding off some bone-deep chill that only she could feel.

It was irrational to think of Dawson as responsible for what had happened, Corrigan would have to admit, but given his rather transparent motivation to make this trip in the first place, how could he not be?

"One thing's for sure," Corrigan told her. "Neither one of us would be here if it weren't for Dawson's political agenda. That's what it comes down to, any way you slice it."

"Even if you're right," Dara said, "you just can't say things like that to Fielding Dawson."

"As a reporter for *USA Magazine,* you mean."

"Exactly," she said. "I could lose my job, Richard. It's as simple as that." She gave him a look, then turned toward the spot where the wranglers had stowed their packs. Corrigan gave a last look Dara's way, then moved for the campfire, where Vaughn was ladling out bowls of soup, which steamed in the chilly air.

CHAPTER

17

By the time they had finished lunch and shouldered their packs—each containing a sleeping bag, water, and other essentials, and the clothes and toiletries they'd all been asked to give over to Donnelly's men back in Jackson for packing—it had begun to drizzle, forcing them all to pause while the packs came off, ponchos retrieved and donned, the packs replaced.

Finally they all were moving again, and so long as the trail cut beneath the pines, the rain reached them as more of a cooling mist than an annoyance. Inside of half an hour, they had broken out of the cover of the pines and were moving up a series of switchbacks toward the ridge overlooking the lake, where, as Donnelly had explained, they would hook on to the trail that led downward. Meantime, Corrigan noted, the rain seemed to have lessened. The clouds, though, had descended from the peaks and settled over the lake like dense fog, masking the view of the distant cliff where the Mallard had crashed.

Just as well, he thought with a last glance over his shoulder. Perhaps with the crash site out of view, something of the gloom that had enveloped them all would disappear as well.

He turned his attention up ahead, where Ben Donnelly stood at one juncture of the zigzagging trail, calling out his version of encouragement as various members of the party passed by. "Okay, this is a tough stretch ahead. Don't overdo it. Rest when you need to. It's not a sprint, it's a marathon. . . ."

Corrigan, who had purposely lagged near the end of the line, glanced up the steep hillside to see that even Elizabeth Dawson and Sonia Ashmead, burdened as they were with packs easily the size of his own, seemed to be holding pace just fine. Dara, too, was up ahead, somewhere out of sight.

Corrigan, already feeling some strain in his thighs, moved past Donnelly, then stopped a few feet up the trail, realizing his breath had quickened considerably.

"It's the altitude," Donnelly said, moving his way. "But don't worry, this part'll be behind us in another half hour or so. You'll get your wind back then."

Corrigan, who'd been careful not to huff and puff when he passed the outfitter, considered kicking the man off the narrow path. Donnelly, however, had paused a few feet below him, well out of booting range.

"Go ahead," Corrigan said, gesturing at Donnelly.

"No can do," Donnelly said, shaking his head. "I'm the last man up the trail. My job."

Corrigan glanced back down the trail toward the tree line. "How about Chipper and Pete?"

Donnelly followed his gaze. "They peeled off a ways back. They'll head over the ridge, catch the alternate trail I was talking about. Straight down the face of Black Mountain."

Corrigan nodded. He stared out along the ridgeline but could see no one.

"There's a fold in the mountain between us and them," Donnelly said, as if he could read Corrigan's thoughts. "You'll be able to see them